Hopeful Christian

Jack Webb

Hopeful Christian

DRIFTER BOOKS
NEW YORK

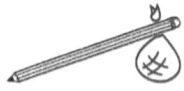

Drifter Books
New York, NY 10034

Cover design, interior design,
and illustrations by Jack Webb

For Theresa.

Who is crazier:
a crazy person, or
the woman who loves him?

"I became insane,
with long intervals of horrible sanity"
—Edgar Allan Poe

". . . wisdom, and folly,
are equal before the face of Infinity,
for Infinity knows them not."
—Leonid Andreyev

Hopeful Christian

My first impulse was to run . . . out the door and far away. My second was to scream—something about how much of a travesty the whole situation was, and how I knew little, if anything, about who was involved, and how *it* got started. Deny all allegations. Deny everything. My third impulse was not so much impulse as it was unmitigated genetic force. A powerful, winning force: seize up and play dead.

As my knees buckled and I crumbled to the floor like so much soft, pink meat, I was thinking, *Jesus. Is that smell me? Did I just shit my pants, or is that just how rooms smell at waist height?*

Immediately, I was given an answer. "Fuck. Did you just shit yourself?"

The man in the doorway fanned air away from his nose. "Fucking shit, man, what's wrong with you? Will you

3

just sign for this package, so that I can leave? I still have a lot of stops to make, and it's getting dark."

Dark? Mother of God. Didn't I just wake up? Wasn't it morning a minute ago?

The postal worker bent down and extended an electronic signature pad to the pile of me lying on the floor. I reached up and scribbled two C's on the glowing screen.

The package was small, square, and brown. A basic box. No frills. He placed it on the ground in front of my face, and then he ran.

I don't blame the guy, I thought, feeling shame slice into my already eviscerated ego. *I'm crazy. A loon. Stark raving mad. And these drugs are not helping. For fuck's sake, what kind of man has a nervous breakdown when the delivery service knocks at the door? Well, at least one: me. Crazy.*

I scooped up the package and held it like a linebacker cradling a football. Only, with the apparent load in my pants, my shuffle to the bathroom was not nearly as graceful. Considering the comparison . . . that was saying something.

Expecting the worst . . . I wiped. *Merciful Mary, I thank you. No shit. I did not go in my pants. Placebo effect. The smell made me think that I had shit. It was only a wet, very wet, swampishly wet fart.*

I had been sweating for hours. When I farted, gas bubbled out from between my moist cheeks like smoke through a water bong. What came out was different, stronger—pure stink.

In my haste to clean myself I had dropped the box, and was surprised when it suddenly caught my gaze; a cube.

How did it get there? Did I put it there? Shit, did it walk? What? What was that noise? A tick? What was that? A tick? What ticked? The box? Did the box tick? Fuck . . . it's probably a bomb. I stared at the box like a man staring at his death.

What should I do? Should I throw it out the window? Open it and try to disarm it? Or, should I just sit back and let it go? Blow me away. It's a miracle I lasted this long. I was due for a bomb package years ago.

The drugs had made me mad. I could not contain my thoughts. They shot out fast and at random. There was nothing about this plain cube to indicate that it was a bomb. I was paranoid. The tick was in my head. I tried to regain control.

Why would I jump to that? A bomb? Pft. Who would want to bomb me? Why would . . . why . . .

"What was that? Did you hear that?" My voice echoed in the small empty room.

Yes.

"It sounded like a tick, didn't it?"

Yes.

Did the voice in my head really hear the tick, or was it just trying to throw me off? Keep me crazy? I did not know. I was far too high to know anything for certain.

"Shut up, you bastard. Quit playing games. My life is at stake." I yelled loud enough for him to know that I meant business, and he fell silent.

"Good. Now be quiet while I investigate." I leaned down from my seated position on the toilet and put my ear to the box.

Suddenly, I was a 220-pound yoga master. The angle of my back was extreme and I had no doubt that it would be red with pain if not for the drugs. I held my breath and listened.

"Nothing. There wasn't any tick."

Yes, there was.

"No."

Yes.

"Quiet, you bastard."

Again, I put my ear to the box. Again, I heard nothing.

"What? Do you think the bomb is going to stop ticking just because I'm listening to it? It wouldn't do that." Uncertain, I added, "Would it?"

I tried to ignore the voice but it was insistent. *Yes. It's trying to trick you.*

"No. It wouldn't do that. It couldn't. Besides, anyone who knows anything knows that bombs don't tick. Everything is digital now. Red glowing numbers."

Apparently seeing the logic of my words, the voice finally quit protesting.

I brought the box to the living room. With it, I sat on the couch and looked out through the room's only window—a clear view of a dirty, red-brick, Manhattan alleyway. Miserable.

Miserable view, but it was the only one we could afford. A faint beam of light shone through the glass and I tilted the label to meet it.

The shakily handwritten text read, "To Christopher Christian," my address, "from Mexico."

No name-of-sender. No street address. Simply "from Mexico."

"Who the fuck?"

The voice came back and said, *You've done too many of their drugs. Smoked, snorted, and eaten too much. Demanded too much. Shrinking the already limited supply. You've thrown off the whole market. Fucked up their business model.*

"That's it. Of course, it's obvious. A fool could see; I'm using more than they are capable of replacing and this makes them feel like ineffective business owners. And if there is one thing the Mexican cartel hates, it is when they are made to feel like they are being ineffective business owners."

I heard something and jumped. This noise did not come from my head or the box. This noise was real.

It was my lifeline. My umbilical cord. The electric portal that connected, plugged me in, kept me in touch with the world.

My phone.

It was Sofia. *Shit.*

"Maintain."

Chapter 2

"Uhh. Hello. Hey, I can't hear you. Are you there? Hello? Are you there?"

No response. Panic gripped me.

Fighting the urge to hang up the phone, I asked again, "Hello?"

"Hey, babe. Jesus, you okay?" On her end I heard the distinctive chime of an MTA train door closing.

Subway. She has bad reception—of course.

"Yeah. Yeah. Yeah. I'm good. I'm good. Everything is good here. How are you? How are you?"

Did I repeat myself? Is there an echo in this room? Am I talking loudly?

"Yes on both counts," she said.

"Huh, what?"

"Yes, you are being loud, and yes, you did repeat yourself."

"Did I say that out loud?"

Obviously concerned she asked, "Say what out loud? Why are you yelling? Are you okay?"

The volume of my voice was beyond my control. "Can't talk now. Doing something. Text me." I screamed the words, ran out of breath, started to cough, and hung up.

The phone vibrated almost immediately. "Jesus, woman. Will you let me breathe?"

The text on the screen read, "Meet me at Dyckman Express in ten minutes."

Dyckman Express was my favorite Dominican restaurant: cheap and with outdoor seating. I was ravenous, and the very thought of Dominican food made my mouth water. I could almost taste the pepper steak.

I was up and dressed in a moment.

As I left, I turned to the package, which was sitting ominously on the couch, and said, "I'll get you. You bastard. I'll get you."

The walk was short—two blocks from my house. On the way I stopped at a sidewalk merchant and bought a belt for my sagging pants. And, for a moment, I even contemplated buying a new pair of pants. Ultimately, I decided against it.

We are spoiled in the city.

Chapter 3

Realizing that I was almost running, I slowed down my steps and thought, *Maintain—she is looking at you.*

"Hey, babe." I kissed her deeply, then suddenly, awkwardly, pulled back. I had been doing drugs all day and had not brushed since the previous night.

I must smell like a Tijuana sweatshop. Yes, I smell it in the air. Soggy drugs, body oil, and must. When was the last time I showered?

"Have you been smoking?" She asked the question but she seemed to know the answer.

"Um. Yes. Ah. A little. Can you smell it? Bad breath?" I palmed my mouth and nose and breathed in and out.

I smelled marijuana but, beyond that? I could not smell anything. I never could. Nobody notices his or her own stink. It always smells natural. It takes the nostrils of others to tell for sure. I thought that I smelled normal, but for all I knew, I reeked.

"No. You smell fine," she said with a chuckle.

"Really? Breath too?" The waitress brought two thick glasses, filled with mostly ice and a little bit of water, to the table. I picked up the one in front of me and swished a few—the only few—cleansing tablespoons of liquid around in my mouth.

"No. Your breath is fine. It's your eyes that give you away. Your eyes are glazed." She smiled and leaned in. "Why didn't you call me?" She paused, looked around cautiously, and then quietly continued, "I would have left work early and smoked with you."

The answer was simple. I wanted to be alone. I could not enjoy my high when she was around. *Right now for example. Point and case.*

"I dunno. It was a quiet morning; I didn't think about it." She looked disappointed at my response. I could see it in her almond-colored eyes. Sadness and longing. I knew the look well.

"Are we going to order food? I'm starving. I could eat a horse . . . "

I smiled, pointed to the menu, and said, "Wait . . . this is a Dominican restaurant. They actually serve horse here. Right? Right? Don't you think?" I smiled at her. "You're Dominican. Don't you know? Point to the horse-meat on the menu. I'll order it."

She smiled and blushed. Embarrassed or angry; perhaps both.

Finally serious, I asked, "How do you say 'steak and onions' in Spanish?"

"Bistec con cebolla." Her words came instantly, automatic and without thought. They tango-danced in her throat and off her tongue with a low growl.

"Bistec con cebolla." I repeated the words wrong.

"Ha-ha. Close." Another smile. She was *so* beautiful. It was more than her obvious physical beauty . . . her personality too. Beautiful. Everything about her was beautiful.

How I managed to find the nicest girl in the city, I would never know.

She looked at me with mild concern and asked, "Are you hot?"

"Huh? What?" The drugs still had me. I was their slave.

"You are sweating. Like . . . a lot." She pointed to my shirt.

I looked down and said, "Jesus." My button-down dress shirt was soaked in the armpits and chest. Wide, dark triangles of sweat in the wrinkled fabric.

The sun was setting and it was barely seventy degrees outside. And . . . I was in the shade. Warm? A little. But I was not hot. This was something else.

Suddenly, I realized that my heart was racing. The table between us warped and stretched. All at once she was miles away.

Her mouth moved but I could not hear her.

"Huh, what?" I asked desperately.

She was too far away. I could not hear her and I could not read lips. I did not know what she was saying.

"I can't hear you," I said.

Again, her lips moved.

"I can't read lips."

She reached with a mile-long arm and grabbed my hand.

The table snapped back to its original size. Again she was only three feet away.

"Why are you yelling? Why would you need to read lips? I didn't say anything." Obviously worried, she asked, "Are you ok?"

"I'm fine." Self-conscious, I lashed out, "Damn it. Don't you see that I'm fine?"

I was lying about being fine. I was not fine . . . I was angry. I had been called out. She knew something was wrong. I was mad that she knew. I was mad that I had been discovered.

Getting to my feet, I said, "I have to go."

"What? We just got here. We haven't ordered food yet. What about your horse?" she said, trying to be—and probably succeeding at being—funny, but I could not bring myself to laugh.

Fear and anger had me. I had to get away.

I had to get back to safety. Back to some place isolated. Back to being alone.

Back, before I exploded. Exploded and an ambulance was needed to suck my juice off the sidewalk, parked cars, pedestrians, and my weeping girlfriend.

"I haven't seen you in a whole day. It feels like forever. I miss you. Baby, I miss you." Her words gave me pause.

I can't just leave, I thought. *I have to give a reason. Something rational.*

At first I could not think of anything; then, it was there.

"I have to go. I need to open a package. I got a package today. I don't know what's in it. It might be perishable." The excuse was flimsy, but it was all I had.

She did not look convinced.

"I'm sorry. I'll call you." I was off before she could respond.

I opened the door to my apartment and shuffled to the kitchen. I grunted and moaned like a beast with every step. The fridge was empty but I still managed to find something to eat. Something old and foul—from the back.

I ate it so quickly that I did not taste it. I did not taste it until it came back up.

I covered the floor in watery puke and collapsed.

I'm fine. I'm fine. I'm not going to die.

The urge to sleep came fast and heavy. I held against it long enough to check my vibrating phone. It was Sofia. Her text read, "I have to meet someone about a new project for work before I can come home. Love you."

I lay on the floor, foaming at the mouth.

I lay on the floor, certain that I would not die.

No, I would not drown in the pinkish puddle of gut waste on the floor. I was certain. Absolutely sure.

Chapter 4

The alarm on my phone went off at four in the morning.

I exploded awake like a soldier waking in a hospital for the first time after a catastrophic injury. *What is this? Where am I? What is this pain? Why can't I feel my legs? The last thing I remember was someone yelling,* "Grenade."

I slapped the phone and it turned off. Again, I went to sleep.

Five in the morning, the alarm began again. I was less surprised this time. Sleep had loosened its grip and some small, logical part of my mind, a part that knew I should get up, was struggling to be the loudest voice in my head—a fool's effort.

I grabbed the phone, dismissed the alarm and placed it next to my head on the bed. "I know I have to get up. I'm practically awake goddammit! I'm just resting my eyes. Relaxing a little before I start my day." I spoke aloud but the voice in my head. . . . he knew I was lying.

"Beep. Beep. Beep." It was six in the morning.

Jesus, I'm going to be late. I jumped out of bed and mad-dashed to the pile of clothes on the living room floor.

Blue undershirt, boxers, black pants, black socks, and company-provided over shirt . . . all dirty. The company shirt was baby blue, elastic cotton, and collared. The left arm said PaperClips and from the left breast hung my nametag.

My nametag: Christopher, Production Associate, and—at the bottom in small letters—in training.

It should have read, "Christopher, worthless pawn." That would have been more accurate.

Written on the bathroom mirror: "Albino A+."

Jesus, who wrote that there? I wondered. *Is that my handwriting?*

The letters were composed of violently sharp angles. Wild whips of what looked to be cherry ChapStick.

Was it me? Is that my handwriting? I can't deal with this now.

The words were undoubtedly a note to myself from the night before. An epiphany I had in the shower that I had to write down lest I forget.

It was a message in a bottle sent from me to me and the words were insane.

Albino A+? Whatever I meant to say, the message

had been lost in translation and I did not have time to try and decode it.

I looked past the letters and at my reflection. My hair was a mess but that did not matter. I had to go.

I wet my hands and flattened a few of the more pronounced cowlicks. Satisfied, I smiled at the man in the mirror. *Handsome devil.*

I was running down my building's cracked marble stairwell when it hit me. *Shit, my book. Do I go back? I'm late as it is. Do I really need it?*

Yes.

I ran back up.

I felt heavy. I was a man in an invisible fat-suit.

My body—and most of my mind—was still asleep. I was running full-auto but the man in the pilot seat with his feet up on the control console still wanted his book. And the man in the pilot seat gets what the man in the pilot seat wants.

I did not turn on a light. I knew where the book was, on the couch, on the center cushion—my reading place. I found it in the darkness and put it into my jacket pocket. Then I was out the door again. As I was leaving, I got a strange feeling.

I sensed something back in my apartment: a monster lurking in the darkness. A savage creature from hell that was ready to pounce. I turned quickly and prepared to fight.

The light from the stairwell shone through the open doorway and into my bathroom. Opposite me on the floor, in front of the toilet, sat the box—unopened.

What are you, you bastard?

I closed the door and left. The drugs, obviously, had not completely worn off.

The A train was only two blocks from my house. I speed-walked and got there in three minutes. It was 6:15 in the morning and the station was already full of people. All types of folks, but mostly Dominicans.

This was a Dominican neighborhood. Dominican-town. It used to be Cuban and before that it was Irish. God only knew whose neighborhood it would be next.

The turnstile dinged as I passed and the train immediately entered the station.

It's 6:15. I might make it to work on time.

Chapter 5

"You're late," said the short, plump, shivering Mexican woman in front of the store. "It is freezing outside. You know how long I've been here? I got here at 6:20. It is now 6:40. Twenty minutes. Twenty minutes in the freezing cold, waiting for you to get here." She was obviously mad.

"Why didn't you just go inside?" I asked, trying to sound funny. I was not.

Pissed, she said, "I couldn't. We need two people to open the store. Company policy. It's a security issue."

"I'm only ten minutes late. We open at 6:30 right?" I was trying to reduce my crime. It did not work.

"We are supposed to clock in at 6:30. That means we should be in the store a few minutes before 6:30, so that we have time to hang up our jackets and get situated before we start working." She said it all at once. No pauses and no breaths. I was impressed.

"My mistake. I'm sorry." I sounded sincere. I was not.

She ignored me and opened the door with a fiery passive-aggression. But the hydraulic resisted, and her show of force looked sad and awkward.

I was reminded of a child who tries to slam a door during a tantrum. Their heart is in it but their body is weak. They try to slam the door, but they barely manage to make it shut.

I followed her into the store. It was bright and the air was thick with the scent of paper and toner.

"Close the door behind you. Make sure it's locked." I nodded to her command and she hurried off behind the registers—into the back.

Welcome to PaperClips. My job. The routine I can't stand. What can I help you find?

Things were becoming toxic here. I had always prided myself on being the square peg in the round hole. The piece that brought chaos to a carefully balanced system.

In the time that I had been working—age sixteen to then: seven years—I had worked at and quit fourteen jobs, and been fired from two. A respectable number to be sure. I approached each job with good intentions. I was always green. Always eager to please. Always insecure.

Always insecure.

Regardless of where I worked or with whom—slobbish imbeciles and intellectuals alike—I wanted acceptance. I was a sniveling, weeping, dog-like creature who lived only to please and needed constant validation. Validation I never received. The more I tried to please those around me, the more I began to resent them.

The resentment would build in me. The voices in my head—insatiably needy characters, the whole lot— would feed each other's psychoses.

"Why don't they like me?" one would ask. "What am I doing wrong?" would ask another. "What's wrong with me? How can I change?"

A voice—black and bitter—would answer: "Change? What? Are you kidding? You're perfect. It's them. Those bozos are to blame. It's not your fault they can't see how great you are. How much they need you."

Then another voice, a rabble-rouser, "Yeah. This place would go to shit if not for you. You work the hardest. You bust your ass. You carry the whole damn place."

Then a voice in the back would scream, "Burn the fucker down. Dance naked in the ashes."

I never burned anything down but the effect was usually the same: total destruction of the workplace.

I would bitch, moan, and find conspirators. I would find the smallest gripes held by my coworkers and balloon them. The conversation would go like this: "Really? Wow, yeah. I totally understand. I agree. It is not your fault. It is *them*. They are to blame. No, you are totally justified in feeling that way. It's on them. They *should* do that. They should and it is your responsibility to complain when they don't. This is a workplace after all. Am I right? We need people to act professionally and do their jobs. It is not your responsibility to pick up the slack. You deserve justice."

I would whip everyone into a frenzy. People would be at each other's throats. Willing and ready to fight and kill. Then when the situation reached a fever pitch, when blood was about to spill, I would quit. I would quit, leaving a wreaked workplace dynamic in my wake. This was how it had gone all my working life, until now.

People move to the city because of opportunity. A strangely persistent belief that all the jobs worth having are in Manhattan and that simply showing up is enough to get someone hired.

This popular myth is why there are so many homeless sulking through the streets, begging for change, and stinking up subway cars. There *are* a lot of jobs in New York City. Some of them, amazing. But there are also millions of people.

A lot of jobs + a lot of people = equilibrium.

The city has a person to job ratio about the same as any place in the world—small towns included.

I graduated from college, moved to the city, and after a period of inactivity started applying for work. My résumé was solid. BA in Visual Arts. Years of working experience: photography studios, production studios, galleries, Dunkin Donuts. A solid résumé.

Four months, twenty-three interviews, and three bribes later I got a job at PaperClips. Part time, nine dollars an hour, and a boss telling me I was lucky. He was probably right.

The toxicity might have been my fault. Based on my history it would be reasonable to blame me, but I was not so sure.

The enormous effort involved in getting this job, mounting bills, and a newly discovered maturity had made me keep my craziness more or less in check. I still bitched. Quite often in fact. But, I now did so through a toothy, thinly drawn smile. And, I had realized that letting others win—talk while I remained silent—did much in the way of easing tensions.

Smile and nod. Offer general phrases of encouragement. Grin like a simpleton. Grin like a kindhearted fool until clock-out and then swear under my breath the whole ride home and a little after. "Filthy bastards. Classless apes. When will they learn?"

Despite my efforts, I recognized the emerging pattern. Small gripes. Things that should not matter suddenly did. Mildly incorrect paperwork, floors not vacuumed, the wrong paper in the Xerox, all suddenly reasons to kill.

Battle lines were being drawn. Militias formed. The morning crew committed psychological warfare as the evening crew called corporate and complained about the smallest infraction.

"No one likes you," said one. "You're doing it wrong," said the other.

Tempers heated. Nothing was getting resolved. Things kept getting worse.

Uncharacteristically, I smiled and nodded.

Chapter 6

The soft-featured Neanderthal—who, judging by his glistening skin and matted hair, had not showered in days—was Cooper. He opened both doors as he exploded into the store. The hinges extended to their limit. Metal crashed against metal. Customers looked, thinking that something had broken. All they saw was Cooper. Fear gripped them. As quickly as they looked, they averted their eyes.

I could see it in their faces: "Don't look at the filthy, door crashing caveman. He'll beg for change. Worse, he might want conversation." They shuffled awkwardly back to their business and I thought, *Judgmental bastards.*

Cooper charged at me like a shark. His eyes and expression were blank. I extended my hand and was met with a crushing, slap-slide handshake. "Hey, Cooper. Another day, another dollar."

"Don't give me that workplace bullshit. Leave that lazy small talk for the corporate cream puffs. We still on for tomorrow?"

I had forgotten we had plans. *Jesus, Sofia will kill me if I skip on another date.*

"Are we still on or what?" He smelled of beer and body odor and I wondered if he was drunk.

He raised an eyebrow and said, "Fuck, man. What is it with you? Are we still on or what?" I said nothing, fumbled with my hands, moved my lips and looked confused. "Perfect. I'll come by your place around nine tomorrow morning."

Shit. Sofia . . .

Cooper disappeared into the back. Then—sensing that it was now safe—six previously hidden customers emerged from the aisles. They pushed together and formed a tight line at the register. It was as if they thought pushing close might make the line move faster. I hated this phenomenon.

Everywhere in the city, wherever there was a line, people were pushing close. Breathing down each other's necks. Intimacy, without payoff. There was no reason for it.

"Did you find everything you needed?" I asked, slowly.

The customer nodded and quickly slid her credit card in the machine. I smiled and shook my head. "You'll have to wait. I haven't scanned your pens yet."

Hours dragged. I cursed life every five minutes and suppressed a frustrated scream every ten. *Damn this place and damn everyone in it. Damn the world. Damn life. Damn, damn, damn.*

A disembodied voice, "Chris!"

"Huh, what?" I asked aloud.

What is that voice? God?

"Chris. Are you serious? I've been calling your name for like two minutes straight."

Hiding my disappointment that it was not God, I said, "Oh. Sorry, Maria. What's up?"

"What, are you tired? It's only eleven."

Painfully aware of the time I responded, "I know. No. I'm good. Why? What's up? Do you need help?"

"Don't worry about me," said Maria in a tone that implied deeper meaning. "I'm good. Just worry about yourself."

Okay?

"Go to lunch. Get it together."

Lunch? Nice. Thank fucking god.

Work, work, work, and then take 40 minutes to yourself. Like most hard working, red-blooded Americans, I loved lunch.

I knew people who smoked, people who drank, and people who ate at lunch. Some kicked up their feet and relaxed. Others took naps. Me? I wrote.

I sat in the PaperClips break room, next to the stalactite farm that doubled as a microwave, wedged against foul-smelling lockers full of unwashed clothing, and under oppressive posters of corporate propaganda. I sat, and I wrote.

Most coworkers thought that I was crazy. Feverishly writing in a diary or something equally emotional and personal. They would never suspect that I had ambitions or that I wanted to be something more. A writer.

To them I was the weakest link. A body. I was a placeholder until they found someone better. I pushed copy on the Xerox machine well enough not to get fired, but that was it. To them I was nothing. I liked it that way. Low expectations meant less responsibility.

Suddenly, Maria's voice interrupted my thoughts and I was forced to stop writing.

"I'm the production expert. Not to mention your boss. I've been doing this for years. I know what I'm doing."

Here we go, I thought as I listened to the conversation in the other room.

"Yeah . . . I don't mean to contradict you, *boss.* But, despite my working here, *I* actually went to college." Cooper went straight for the throat.

Their voices were only thinly veiled behind the whir of printers and machinery. I could hear them clearly from the break room.

Cooper continued, "You might have been at this for a while, but I know a thing or two myself. BCIM Gloss card stock should be set as 'Coated Two' in the printer. 'Coated One' is for eight-point gloss and Allure. The rollers just don't . . ." He was cut off.

Maria was getting defensive. "Listen. I know what I'm talking about. I know a lot. I may not have gone to college, but I still made it this far."

"Yeah? And just how far is that? PaperClips?" I could hear Cooper clapping. "Congratulations, Maria."

Muffling a laugh, I thought, *Wow. This dude is a dick.*

"You know what, Cooper? You do it. Do whatever you want." The conversation ended and I began to write feverishly. My lunch was to end in five minutes and I suddenly had a lot of new material.

The day, as always, continued to drag.

Motions. Going through the motions. Over and over. My mind blanked and my body zombied on until 2:30 in the afternoon. The end of my shift. Freedom.

When I left Cooper was waiting for me in front of the store smoking something with a strange smell.

"It's salvia," he said without me asking.

"Damn, really? I hate that stuff. How are you still standing? Salvia makes me feel like my skin is falling off. I have to sit when I smoke that shit."

"That's because you're a pussy. All it does is give me a small buzz."

"Cool," I said over my shoulder as we began to walk—not wanting to dignify the insult of a man high on salvia.

Hopeful Christian

The A train—the blue line on New York City subway maps—was our train. We slid our cards, shimmied through the turnstiles, and made our way to the tracks. It was crowded. A lot of people got off at this time of day. 2:30–3:00 in the afternoon was apparently the end of a lot of morning shifts. Not to mention the standard school day.

Tired, short-tempered, blue-collar workers mixed with teens fresh out of high school. Greasy freaks dripping hormones, both.

A volatile situation. Tired workers, the homeless, rowdy teens, crazies, and the two of us, all jammed into a bouncing tin can.

I ignored the elbow in my back and the breath on my neck. I closed my eyes. I tried to breathe shallowly. The smell was foul. Someone needed a shower. Probably a few someones.

Cooper was looking at me. Wild eyes. Aggressively confrontational. "Chris. You see that guy over there? He's staring at me."

I did not look. "What? He's probably crazy."

Still looking at the stranger he continued, "Or a fag."

"Don't entertain him."

"Look at him. Jesus. The nerve. He's staring right at me. He's not even *trying* to hide it."

"Stop it. You're going to get us killed."

"Look at him. If he sees both of us staring at him he'll back down."

I stared at my feet. "No. I'm not looking."

"Queer."

Chapter 7

As usual, our apartment was empty when I got home. Two people lived there. The evidence was everywhere. Two styles. Two distinct sets of possessions. Panties and bras mingled with boxers and undershirts on the floor. Perfume and fragrant hair products—curling gel, straightening cream, and exotic conditioners—waged an aerial battle with man musk and body spray. Present everywhere was an obvious duality.

Sofia was a ghost in that apartment. I felt her presence, but saw her only on the rarest of occasions and even then, I usually wondered if it was only a dream.

In college—where we met—she was, as she was now, an overachiever. For me college was a binge. A twenty-four-hour, seven day a week party that occasionally paused in the form of a class. I did well enough. I passed. Sofia? She won.

For her, college was a serious matter—an early extension of her career. I did not realize it then, but while I was worried about sex, beer, and the occasional take-home assignment, she was worried about getting a job, making connections, and, amazingly, long term goals.

When we graduated and decided to move to the city together this trend continued. She hit the ground running. Each day for her held a new project, meeting, and connection. She feverishly sent out résumés and cover letters while I got feverish from cheap hooch and various vapors.

Five months later, money was getting tight. Student loan spillover was running out and I felt the need for employment. At this point Sofia was neck deep in a budding career. Me? I was just beginning. My motivation? Beer money. I did not know how difficult it would be to make it in the city. I thought I could take my time. I did not feel the need to rush into it. I was wrong. Sofia had been born and raised in Manhattan. As a local she knew what it took to be successful in her community. She knew to network, work hard, and hustle. She had been doing it since college. She had been doing it all her life.

While I sat in our musty apartment nursing paper cuts and a bruised ego she was out looking nice, acting nice, and playing hard. While I sat tired and sick, she was out working hard, and making connections that would stick.

I knew she would make it. I had no doubt that she would achieve all of her dreams. She had a good job. She would contribute to her field and feel the deep pride that comes with success. She would smell the city air and know that if it gave her lung cancer she could afford the resulting medical bills. She would buy a condo, the biggest television available, and a closet full of fashionable shoes. She would be known far and wide and she would be proud. She should be proud. She deserved it.

Chapter 8

Slam.

The sound of a door closing woke me. Frantic and disoriented, I groped at Sofia's side of the bed. Empty. Empty but still warm.

Something crisp on her pillow. Something cold. A sheet of paper. I grabbed it, squeezed it in my fist and held it to my chest.

In moments I was out of bed, down the hall, and in the bathroom. Puke. The flow was hot and thick. Pink toilet water jumped and splashed as new waste mixed with old within the dirty bowl.

Wiping my mouth I mumbled, "I got up too fast. Or, I drank too much last night."

Likely it was a combination of both.

Finally, I straightened and read the paper. It was a letter from Sofia, short yet apologetic. She did not want to wake me—"because I looked so peaceful"—but she was called in to work. No mention was made of our scheduled date.

Did she forget?

My phone chimed in the other room and I staggered towards it. "Hello?"

My breath was toxic. The sharp, vinegar smell of stomach acid filled the air. Again, I felt the urge to puke. The urge was strong but I tried hard to resist.

Despite myself, muscles involuntarily contracted in my throat causing me to gag—loudly.

A voice on the line asked, "Choking? What I tell you about sucking dick?"

"What's up, Cooper?"

"We still on for today or what?"

I tried to reply but my words were intercepted by another gag.

"Don't tell me . . . you have a date with your old lady? Shit, Chris. If I'da known you had such a big vagina, I would have bought flowers and condoms for today instead of this case of beer."

I wiped my mouth and said, "Nice . . . I'll meet you there in an hour. Bring the beer. I'll buy the gummy worms."

Cooper was already there when I arrived. Sitting on the Hudson's rocky shore, he already had five empty cans of Budweiser strewn on the ground around him. Thirsty, I quickened my pace to meet him.

"Cooper, already drunk?"

Without looking back he began reeling in his fishing line. "You got the gummy worms?"

"Yeah. I do. Did you save me any beers?"

He pointed to a large gym bag perched on a large chunk of Manhattan schist. The bag was wet and dripping. I watched as a droplet rolled to a stop and clung to a clear piece of mica. The two shone brightly in the warm morning sunlight.

"I brought a whole twenty-four pack. I also brought ice so before you start bitching maybe you should . . . "

I cut him off. "You're using a candy bar wrapper as bait?"

"What the hell else you expect me to use? I was waiting for you to bring the good stuff."

"Couldn't you have . . . I don't know . . . dug around and tried to find a real worm?"

"You know as well as I do that city fish don't eat normal fish food. Damn things live in the lap of fucking luxury. Fuck, I've been out here thirty minutes and I've already seen three bags of chips, a soda bottle, and a happy meal bag float by. Why would a fish go for worms when they can just as easily get a hamburger and fries?"

I threw him the pack of sugar-worms and grabbed a beer. The day was crisp and a thin layer of dew still clung to grass wherever there was shade.

I watched as Cooper guided a thin silver hook in and through a yellow, green, and red worm. With the bait set, he reeled back and cast his line like someone trying to throw a football. Not surprisingly, the hook landed no more than ten feet away.

"With light bait you need a gentler cast. Try swinging from the hip next time."

He looked at me scornfully and said, "The day I take advice on how to cast from a Yankee is the day I tuck my dick in my ass and start singing show tunes."

I snickered and set my own line. "Let me show you how it's done. It's all in the wrist."

A flick from the hip and my line was out nearly three times as far as his. He was not impressed.

Reeling in his line for another attempt he said, "You owe me ten dollars for the beer."

I watched as the current began to pull my line downstream—towards a forest of water-worn wooden beams—and asked, "Why are we over here on the rocks instead of over there on the pier?"

"Dominicans. A shit-ton of them over there barbecuing."

"Already? This early?"

"Still. By the looks of them I'd say they'd been here all night."

Still surprised, I asked, "So? It's not like you to accommodate anyone, let alone drunk strangers."

He opened another beer. "I don't fuck with Dominicans around here. Back on the street is one thing. Down here? Around these parks? Fuckers get territorial. Damn near got the shit beat out of me the first week I moved here. I didn't know anything about the neighborhood or the people. Walked about like I owned the place. Until this one night . . . here I was, drunk off my ass and walking home . . . "

He finished his newly opened beer, grabbed another, opened it, began to drink, and then—after a long swig—he continued, "Used my phone for navigation, so I wasn't paying no attention to where I actually was. So drunk and oblivious I didn't even hear that shitty Dominican music blasting all around me. Turns out it was a Dominican holiday or some shit. Before I knew it, a bunch of drunk dudes in Dominican flag T-shirts start hassling me about being in their neighborhood. I push them, they push back. Long story made short . . . I'm nursing a bloody nose and some bruised ribs."

"So now you just submit?"

"Who's submitting? Only an idiot starts trouble behind enemy lines."

"I can't tell you how ironic it is to hear you say that. Of all the people . . . you're the last person I'd expect to do the calm and rational thing."

Cooper looked at me with an expression that was a mixture of rage and disbelief. "What the fuck you trying to say? You trying to say I'm stupid? You trying to say I'm fucking stupid."

Disbelief gone. He stood and was all rage. I rose to meet him.

"Cooper. Your reel is being pulled into the water."

"The fuck?"

Jack Webb

He was knee deep in the Hudson before he caught up to his fishing rod.

Chapter 9

Now, for some background . . . my childhood was foul beyond words. This is not a complaint, but fact. I have neither the ability nor desire to explain so I will not even try.

I left home almost the day I turned eighteen. That was when things started to change.

At first I was wild, rebellious, stupid—worse, I was unseasoned. I was a flavorless copy of the hippie archetype. True to form, I puked ideology, grew out my hair, and indulged myself.

Unleashed on an unsuspecting campus, I spent most of my first semester in college seducing dorm rats and getting high. College was a playground. I would steal marijuana from my drug dealer roommate and smoke out on the soccer field. I never went to class. I thought that I had forever to make the grade. I would get around to it . . . eventually. I was making up for lost time—years wasted. I was stupid. I did not care. Not at all. Not until I ate mushrooms.

Psilocybe cubensis are a type of mushroom that contains psilocybin. Psilocybin is converted by the body to psilocin. Like LSD, psilocin affects the brain in a powerful way. A few nibbles of the mushroom will make your body comfortable. A few more makes the world beautiful. A maximum dose results in a religious experience. God is seen in whatever form you require.

The first time I tried them I had no idea what to expect. I did not do the research. Like I said . . . I was stupid. Thankfully.

I conned a greasy weirdo into buying the mushrooms. "Yeah, man. Just give me forty dollars and I will get you some. Simple as that." He gave me the money and I got the stuff. I got the stuff and took half the bag for myself.

I explained, "The bag might feel light, but that's because this is the good shit. When it's good they give you less. It's fine. Don't worry about it. You don't need much. Why? I told you. What, are you stupid? It is the good shit. What, you don't trust me?" I was lying about the price but my assessment of the quality was dead on. Much to my surprise.

We were at a party off campus. The apartment belonged to a student I had never talked to. Never even seen. I knew no one but my tripping buddy.

The smoky room began to look bright through my aviator sunglasses. I popped the collar on my tropical print button-down and sat in a corner. The group seemed to be moving at light speed. Pulsating pillars. Back and forth. Back and forth. Back and forth. I could smell the sweat.

"I think I feel it," I said, out loud to myself.

"Me too. I'm totally tripping."

My associate had been gone for what seemed like hours and the suddenness of his words startled me. "Jesus, man, where did you come from?" I asked.

"I went to get a beer. I was only gone for a second. Are you okay? What do you feel?"

"I dunno. Pillars and vibrations."

He sat down next to me. "What? That's weird. I'm not really seeing anything. I mean, things are bright, kinda, but . . . "

I cut him off. "I'm not sure I like it. I think I took too much."

"Calm down, man. It's all good. Relax and let go."

"What? You're not the boss of me. You can't tell me what to do."

"What the fuck are you talking about?"

I got to my feet. "You want me to fucking punch you?"

"What the fuck, man?"

"I need to get out of here. This place is getting to me. I can't take it. I need to get out."

I ran.

The journey back to campus was hellish. In the dark I could hear and see everything. Buildings grew and towered overhead, menacingly. The road shrank and stretched under my feet. Laughter, music, and cars echoed in the distance, but thankfully not on the road I was on. That road was empty.

Campus was on a hill. I approached it like a man approaching the holy land. Its bright lights and significance blinded and overwhelmed me. Suddenly I could not advance.

"Jesus, what is wrong with me?" I yelled into the darkness.

I found a baseball field just off campus. It was a wide-open space behind a public high school. The field was lush and beautifully green. Behind home base was a tall half-dome fence. I felt an overwhelming urge to climb to the top and did not fight it.

The night was hot and the metal was cold. Refreshing. I clanged to the top and spread out on my belly. I shoved my face into the chain link and looked out the corner of my eye. The glowing fortress of knowledge on the hill shone down on me like heaven and suddenly I realized that it was.

"What am I doing? Why am I wasting this opportunity? So much of my life has already been wasted. I can't afford to fool around. College is a place for new beginnings. I can start over. Be better. Go to class and try to pass. Stop burning the locals. Try monogamy. And . . . quit being so hard on myself."

Tears flowed on that late summer night. I sat there for hours, talking to my new and old friend, the fence.

Lying there pressed against its geometric pattern—

its rational beauty—I changed. Hours later I descended. Reborn.

The next day I cut my hair and went to class. Eventually I graduated from college.

That fateful day could have gone differently. I could have stuck with marijuana.

Chapter 10

My coworker, Alejandro, was a filthy, fat freak, and I hated him. Snooty bastard. Patronizing sack of obesity. He made me sick. Sick to the core. In front of PaperClips, I greeted him with a smile.

"Hey Alejandro! Cold this morning, huh?"

He replied with a raised eyebrow and a dismissing smirk. Nothing verbal.

"Back to work, huh? Another day, another dollar. Cooper told me he wasn't going to be here today. I didn't know he got you to cover. I'm excited. You and I never get to work together."

Still nothing. I began to scream in my mind. *Rude. Disrespectful swine. Say something. Do you think I want to do this? Lowering myself to idle conversation. Shooting the shit with your stupid skull matter. This is painful. An extreme effort. I hate debasing myself like this. Give me something.*

I decided to change my tactics. "This place, right? Shit, what a mess," I said, motioning to the locked doors of our store.

"Yeah." *He speaks. Finally . . . a word.*

Sipping his coffee he continued, "I'm going to write a sitcom about this place."

Surprised, I asked, "Really?"

"Yeah, I have a lot of ideas." He pointed to me and smiled. "Especially about your character."

Especially my character? What the hell does that mean?

He took another loud sip of his coffee, and then said, "Yeah, it's going to be a comedy."

Hesitant, I said, "Cool."

"Yeah."

"You write a lot?"

"Yeah."

"Do you think you're any good?"

"Yeah."

Interest peaked I asked, "Really? I love reading, you should let me take a look at some of your stuff." No response. "I'd love to read something. Honestly, I would really like to read some of your work."

"I don't think *you'd* like it." He put heavy emphasis on the "you'd." I stared at him blankly. He nodded and continued, "I have a sophisticated style. The things I write about are highbrow."

Sophisticated. Really? Like comedies set at PaperClips.

You fat fuck. I hate you, Alejandro.

"Umm. Okay. O.K., sure." I smiled at the pig, nodded and contemplated the consequences of homicide.

I hated waiting in front of the store. If I lived and worked someplace else, anywhere else, it might not have been so bad, but there, in the city, it was torture. It was six in the morning and the street was already crowded. Joggers, dog walkers, commuters, paperboys, papermen, the homeless filled the sidewalk. No one slept in that town.

Every minute or so a consumer—someone who absolutely must buy pens and PaperClips at six in the morning—would bump into me as they tried to get into the store, always with the same result: they pushed past, grabbed the door handle and jerked it violently. When it did not open they looked at the posted store hours and walked away in disgust.

Occasionally one would ask me—always in a venomous and judgmental tone—"Do you work here?"

To which I replied, "Nope. I am just loitering."

Sometimes they came back and tried to confront me about it. "I thought you said you didn't work here?" I pretended not to know what they were talking about and apologized profusely for any misunderstanding. "It was dark. I understand. It is not your fault. I have one of those faces."

I felt as though I was on display. Waiting in front of the store in my uniform, I felt like a manikin. An advertisement. A warning about the effects of trying to pursue a professional career in the arts.

In my mind, children would pass and point. "Look,

mommy. Look at the loser. He works at PaperClips. He thought he could do something with a BA in Visual Arts."

The child's mother would shake her head mournfully. "Yes. He was foolish, sweetie. Let that be a lesson to you. You're going to get a degree in business. Right?"

"Yes I am, mommy. I want to be successful. I won't be a loser like him."

I wanted to die. I wished that the manager would come and let me in. Free me from the humiliation.

The sun had not yet begun to creep over the jagged skyline and it was cold. Back home—in upstate country—I imagined a deer quietly walking through the woods. Lazily enjoying the last few minutes of night. Enjoying the brief reprieve from the human menace.

I envisioned him savoring a wild berry—a straggler that had managed to hang on this far into fall. Slowly chomping what might be his last meal before the wild country boys, with shaved heads and red necks, woke up and tried to kill it.

Here? There is no such thing as quiet. No alone time. I'm forced to be social.

Forcing myself to be social I spoke, "I dabble in writing."

Seemingly uninterested in conversation, Alejandro breathed a soft, "Huh?"

"I said that I dabble in writing."

"What?"

Pull the fat folds off from your ears, and listen.

"I write," I repeated. "I'm a writer."

"What do *you* know about writing?"

"I know a few things."

Alejandro lifted his nose slightly and seemed to be sniffing at the sky. "Well. It is difficult, you know. Being a writer takes talent and determination, to say nothing of creative intelligence."

"Um, I guess." *How long would I spend in jail if I punched your teeth out right here and now? Do I even care? Would I be any worse off? Probably not.* Resisting the urge to grind my teeth, I continued, "Right now I'm working on my voice. I am trying to find it. Narrow in on it. I've had a general sense of my style all my life—as I am sure everyone does. But now I am really focusing on perfecting it. Making my voice as distinct and fully developed as possible."

"What are you talking about?"

"My voice . . . " He looked at me in a way that made me feel stupid. "My voice," I insisted. "My own special way of writing. My style. Prose. For example . . . I like short sentences. I tend to use fragments. I like that though. I like how it sounds. It is like poetry."

"I never think about that. Only people who have to *try*—those without natural talent . . . only they have to think about such trivial things. I just *do*. It comes naturally to me. I don't have to think about it."

I was starting to crack. *I'll kill him, I swear.* Defensive, I asked, "Have you ever been published? I mean if you are so talented . . . surely, you must have published something."

He appeared to be growing angry and his calculated way of speaking was degrading. As it did his Spanish accent became more pronounced. He began to lisp. It was a heavy lisp that reminded me of a cartoon from my childhood. A cartoon pig. Or maybe cat. I could not remember which.

His words began to run together. No pauses. Each sentence sounded like a long word. "No. I write many things. Many thoughts. Always, I am writing. One day I will sit down and put it all together."

"One day?"

"Yes. Did I stutter?" He spat as he talked. His throat and lips were loose from countless gorge sessions. Chickens swallowed whole.

Five minutes of awkward silence later, Maria emerged from a black taxi and said, "Sorry I'm late."

"Don't worry about it. Alejandro and I had a nice conversation." She did not look convinced. Alejandro stared coldly in my direction. My mask was practiced. I was all smiles.

The day blurred past. I felt like a hamster in a wheel. Running in place. Frantically, I worked at achieving nothing. Just another gear in the machine. Just another small piece. Just another loser.

Before I knew it, I was home, tired, and getting ready for bed. Which was good because I needed to go to bed early. I needed my rest. I had to wake up on time. I had work in the morning.

Chapter 11

59th Street, Columbus Circle was, in my opinion, the most beautiful place in Manhattan. It was what I imagined when I closed my eyes and thought of New York.

It was not normally crowded there. At least not Times Square crowded. Tourists seemed to bypass it.

Columbus Circle was not as famous as Rockefeller Center, Times Square, or the Statue of Liberty; that might have had something to do with it.

The Time Warner building, while ridiculously beautiful—again, in my opinion—did not roll off the tongue like the "Chrysler Building" or have the unmitigated machismo of the "Empire State Building."

The roundabout was beautiful. Glass monoliths and

Central Park encircled a monument to the most famous explorer ever to get lost on his way to the East Indies— Christopher Columbus. Columbus stood high atop a naval-themed podium. From the ground the view up his nostrils was magnificently unobstructed.

Broadway, 8th Avenue, and 59th Street intersected here. A traveler could get anywhere in Manhattan from Columbus Circle. Walk up 8th, past the Museum of Natural History, through the Upper West Side, and eventually you would reach the Heights. Walk down Broadway and there you would be . . . Downtown. SoHo, and past SoHo, the Lady Liberty.

Walk 59th crosstown and you would find everything in-between: Midtown.

The only thing missing was a straight line from there to the Upper East Side. For that, one would have to walk a path through Central Park—a pleasant failing, to say the least.

Before and after work, I liked to go to the Circle. I liked to sit at the corner, the outer edge of the roundabout, at Columbus's back, on the rounded southwest edge of Central Park.

Twice a day, every day. I would go and I would sit. Amongst marble statues and passersby I would sit and think. Mostly I thought about how much I hated life.

I would arch my back, tilt my chin straight up, and look at the glass skyscraper across the way. Tall, sleek, shiny, and a bitch. She taunted me. She taunted the shit out of me. But I loved her still.

That building was where *it* happened. It was where

the smart and ambitious heavyweights of media hung their hats and worked their nine-to-fives. Where they made all the important decisions. At least that was what I imagined.

Lucky shmucks.

I saw ten celebrities out in front of that building a day. Not that I cared about such things. I honestly did not.

What interested me? The people I was interested in were the producers, writers, and directors. The bosses. The creative and technically tuned brains that gave pretty faces their lines, told them where to stand and where to look.

They were there. Behind that one-way, mirrored glass. *Are they looking down at me? Can they see me looking at them? Are they used to the view?*

What really got my goat? What really ground my gears and put my panties in a bunch? Knowing that—in addition to offices full of workers—there were apartments behind that glass.

People actually live in this building, I thought.

I was jealous. Painfully jealous. I ached for enough disposable income to be able to afford such lavish accommodations.

What is it like to wake up each morning to an aerial perspective of Central Park? Does the sight make them cry? Do they have time in their presumably busy lives to look? Have they grown used to that view, too?

Behind a section of that glass, somewhere high above my head, a rich someone was dropping a rose-scented turd into what I could only assume was a solid gold toilet.

Abruptly, I sucked down a savage whoosh of air. I had not been breathing. *Jesus. When was the last time I took a breath?*

"What? Who? Oh? No. I am fine," I said.

The stranger sitting next to me on the marble bench looked concerned. "Your cheeks are blue," she said.

"Are they?" I smiled at her. It was my nicest and most sincere smile. The smile I reserved for first dates and kind strangers. She blushed. Her cheeks pinked and her gaze dropped shyly to the ground.

"It is . . . " My brain grasped for something to say. "I'm blue . . . " Still catching my breath I said, "It is cold outside . . . thank you for your concern, though."

"No problem. I'm just glad I don't have to call an ambulance."

"A lot of people wouldn't even do that much. It's nice to meet someone genuinely kind."

"No. Someone would have called. I'm sure of it. People are good. I'm sure of it." Her words had a strange wispy quality. As if they were not meant for me to hear. She seemed to be trying to convince herself.

"My name is Chris."

The beautiful stranger looked at me, crossed her legs, and arms, then said, "Hello, Chris. You live here in the city, don't you?"

"How could you tell?"

"No camera. That's a big give away."

"Yeah," I said and smiled again.

She was quickly getting used to me. She looked comfortable. Excited, but comfortable.

I pointed to her large blue purse and said, "You don't have a camera either. Do you live here?"

"No. I've just never been much of a picture taker."

"You're a tourist?"

"Yeah. Guilty. You caught me."

"What are doing here in the city?"

She shrugged and said, "People watching."

"People watching? Well, there are certainly a lot of people around here. Still . . . I hope you didn't travel far. People are, more or less, the same wherever you go." *Except for those flower farting freaks who live up in the top floors of that building across the way. Those bastards with the gold toilets. They* are *different, by God.*

She shrugged again but said nothing.

I continued, "Honestly though? People watching? I hope you didn't travel far. I'm not one for judging the hobbies of strangers, but people watching seems like a weird reason to come to Manhattan."

She laughed and said, "Ha-ha. Yeah. No. People watching is what brought me to this park bench. My boyfriend is what brought me to the city."

"Oh, you have a boyfriend?" I sounded disappointed. I was.

She turned bashful again. We broke eye contact. She looked at the ground and played with a pebble under her foot.

"Yeah. My boyfriend wanted to visit the city. We drove here last night."

"Where is he now?"

"He's out exploring."

"Why are you not with him?"

"I've been here before. I was actually born here."

"Really?" I asked.

"Yeah. So . . . I've already seen the sights."

"So you just ditched him."

"We got into a fight." She tensed in a way that was visible. I read surprise on her face. She seemed surprised at her forwardness. I could tell she was not used to talking about her problems.

Trying to sound empathetic I said, "Relationships: they can be hard sometimes." I felt a sudden need to play counselor.

Her rigidity softened and she said, "Try all the time."

"Having troubles?"

"Not him. I am, though. I guess. A little."

"Nothing serious?"

"I don't even know." She paused, then continued, "We've been together for so, so long. Everything he does . . . " She shook her head as if trying to avoid a foul smell. "Everything he does makes me mad. It's not him, though. He is a good guy. Honest. He just pisses *me* off."

She looked at me and I could see a pained kind of sincerity in her eyes. She bit her bottom lip then, after a few quick nibbles, she continued, "The things he says. The way he says them. He opens his mouth and I cringe."

I let out a gentle chuckle and said, "This is so funny."

"What is?"

"This. This whole conversation. I am going through the same thing."

"You have a girlfriend?" Now, she looked uncomfortable, and she sounded disappointed.

I thought for a moment, trying to remember when Sofia and I first started dating, and then said, "Yeah. Three years last month."

"You sound like a prisoner."

"What?"

She began slowly, "I mean you sound like . . . I dunno. You sound how I imagine a prisoner might sound when asked how long he's been locked up." She panto-mimed a prisoner counting lines on a cement wall and said, "Three years. Eight months and eighteen days tomorrow at noon."

More than a little impressed by her acting skills, I smiled and asked, "What? You're not going to go down to the minutes and seconds?"

"He's a prisoner, not a genius."

We both laughed loudly and passersby gawked at us.

I wiped a tear from my eye and said, "This conver-sation . . . how bizarre."

"What?"

I pointed to the two of us and said, "We are having a heart-to-heart. Two complete strangers."

"Yeah. Is that weird?"

I nodded in reply.

She smiled. "How long have you lived here in the city?"

"A little more than a year."

"In that time, I'm sure you've met your share of crazies."

I opened my eyes wide and spoke with all the seriousness I could muster, "More than my share. It's like they are attracted to me. They see me and home in. Attack."

She bobbed her head enthusiastically and said, "See? That's my point. In a city of eight million people you were bound to meet at least one good one."

"I guess statistically I would have to. Still it is ironic that out of millions of people the only nice one I can find is you—a visitor."

"Well . . . " She spoke bashfully, "You are nice. That makes two. See? Our numbers are growing by the second."

It was my turn to be bashful. I felt my cheeks get warm and I imagined that they were glowing.

Looking into her eyes I said, "What a strange meeting this is."

A few silent moments passed between us. It was a comfortable silence. A silence shared by old friends.

She pointed to my upper body and said, "You want to know how I really knew that you weren't a tourist? Your clothes. That's how."

Puzzled, I asked, "My clothes?"

"They're working clothes."

I looked down at myself. I was wearing a light jacket, but my PaperClips nametag was easily visible behind the jacket's half-zipped zipper.

"Your shoes. Boots are not good for touristing. Most tourists sport sneakers. Still . . . what really gave you away was your expression. Tired, unamused . . ."

"Sad?" I asked.

"I was going to say bored. The look of anyone fresh out of work." She paused and I got the sense that she thought the conversation had gone too far. She seemed to be wondering if she was being too familiar with the stranger on the park bench. Her eyes shifted as she backtracked to safe territory in her mind. I could actually see her reeling it in.

"I dunno. The look of a local," she said finally.

"Sometimes I think I *am* a tourist." Unlike her I was not shy. I took a deep breath and continued, "That I am just passing through."

"To where?" she asked.

"I dunno."

"I mean . . . once you've lived in New York City, where else is there left to go? It all seems like a step down."

"What about *you?* You left." My words seemed to hurt her and she looked at her shoes. I looked at her face. I saw regret.

"I just want to be where I am happy," I said.

She nodded and said, "I can understand that."

We paused. She understood. And so did I.

I had spoken without thinking, and by doing so I had released a personal and secret truth. A divine Freudian slip. *I want to be happy. I am not happy. I am unhappy . . . dear God . . . I am so unhappy.*

I could tell that my words had awakened a similar realization within her. Suddenly. Improbably. We were two strangers in sync. Totally in sync.

I caught her gaze and for a time—I was not sure how long—we stared. There was no tension; no urge to look away. Nothing about this moment was awkward.

"Hey, babe." Our trance was suddenly broken by a voice that she seemed to recognize, and after several heavy blinks, turned to confront.

The young man approached us quickly and said, "Hey. Who is this?"

"Oh? Oh. This is . . . " I cut her off and extended a hand.

"My name is Chris." He smiled, grabbed my outstretched hand and squeezed it aggressively. I smiled and returned the sentiment.

"Chris. This is my boyfriend, Jack." She turned to Jack and said, "Chris lives here in the city."

Seemingly uninterested, Jack said, "Oh, really . . . cool. Must be a lot of fun." I smiled a big fake one and told him that it was.

Introductions made, he seemed eager to leave. Impatiently, Jack asked, "Are you ready to go?" He pointed to the Time Warner building and I felt sick. "I want to go into that tall glass building over there." Before she could reply, he turned and started to leave.

"I'll see you later, Chris." She stood and I struggled to think of something to say.

Her eyes begged me to say something—and quick. *I'm trying, damn it.*

"Have . . . uhh. I umm . . ." I fumbled my words. The pressure was enormous. I began to sweat.

I cleared my throat and began again, "Enjoy your time in the city."

She smiled and said, "You too."

Then, she turned. She walked away. She was gone.

Girlfriend of Jack, Ms. One-in-eight-million, you never told me your name.

I looked at the clock on my phone and began to grieve.

Work in ten minutes. Fuck my life.

Chapter 12

"I'm sick," I insisted, overpowering the angry voice on the phone. "Believe me. No one is more upset about this than I am. I need the hours. I have . . ." I paused mid-sentence and forced a loud, hoarse cough. "I have bills to pay," I continued. "I can't afford to . . ."

"Fine," Maria barked. "I'll cover for you." The call was terminated at her end. I was not surprised. She had infinite patience for the customers, but all of us—her coworkers—were simply in her way.

I dropped the phone from my ear and held it by my side as I passed PaperClips. Briefly glancing through the store's glass façade, I could see Maria running around in the production area. Rushing. Waiting. Rushing. Waiting. Rushing. Waiting. Rushing. Dashing. Chasing a finish line that continued to pull farther and farther away—forever.

She is such a fucking joke, I thought and smiled to myself as I continued on my way. The morning was crisp, and the thin, clean air seemed to strengthen me with every breath. I felt alive, new, vital, and thirsty. Thirsty for tomorrow. Thirsty for success. And just plain thirsty. Thirstier than I had ever been. Luckily, I knew a Russian bar down between Eighth Avenue and Broadway that opened early.

"Are you writing your memoirs?" The question sounded distant and reedy. Like a dispatch sent over shortwave radio. I lifted my heavy head and focused my bloodshot eyes in the direction of the unexpected inquiry.

A tall, thin-waisted, fat-faced, blonde Russian woman smiled at me intently. She was beautiful. I immediately wanted to kiss her.

Her pupils were wide, and lined with a thin sliver of puritan gray. Her pigmentless skin was nearly translucent, and, for a fleeting moment, I wondered if it tasted like milk. And, oh, God . . . would she allow me to take a sip from her slender neck?

"No," I said through an acidic, burning hiccup. "I'm a Novelist."

"Really?" She asked the question slowly—taking her time as she pulled her barstool closer to mine. "Can I read your books? Where can I get a copy?"

I had never actually published a book, and now a beautiful woman was calling my bluff. I needed to think up a lie. And quick. A woman as picturesque as she would not wait long for me to respond. She did not have to. She had her pick of any man in the bar, but, for me, this was my only audition for the part of: Lover.

"You can buy them online," I lied.

"What's your name?" She pulled out her phone. "I'll buy a book right now."

Think, damn it, I thought. *She's beautiful. Don't blow this.*

I smiled and tried desperately not to cover her in my beer-blemished breath. "How do I know you're not a stalker?" I asked. "How do I know this . . ." The hiccup was powerful, and I began to choke. "How do . . . do I know this . . . seemingly innocent encounter isn't actually part of some elaborate trap. For all I know, you are planning to kidnap me and lock me in your basement until I write you your *perfect book.*"

She smiled, and said, "You don't . . . ." Then she leaned closer to me and ran her hand through my messy, greasy hair.

The button on my blue jeans groaned and threatened to pop off. It was then when I realized that my bladder was filled well beyond maximum capacity. If I did not piss soon—*soon, soon*—my bladder would undoubtedly explode.

And, instead of sex, I would suffer a violent, stinking, salty, yellow death.

I sprang from the barstool and excused myself. "Make sure nobody puts anything into my drink." I said to her with a wink and a cheeky smile.

While walking down the long, old, oaken bar, I looked back over my shoulder. The beautiful, fat-faced blonde was giggling and speaking in Russian with a group of female friends. Beyond them was the exit. Through the glass and cast-iron door, I could see that the world outside was dull and painted in shades of grey and yellow. The sun had set, and, in its absence, the streetlights had activated and begun to glow their sickly glow.

Jesus, I thought. *What time is it?*

I plucked the phone from my pocket, pressed the *home* button, and looked at the time. Ten o'clock at night. *Where did the time go?* I wondered. *Have I really been here for the entire day?*

I approached a giant, black, grand piano, and all my questions evaporated into the already thick, vodka scented air. On the narrow tip of the piano was a tall, glass vase. It was completely filled with one, five, and ten-dollar bills. A lone twenty lay, wrinkled and torn, on top of the pile.

I reached into my pocket and dropped three singles into the container. "Thank you." The pianist spoke the words with a Russian accent—an accent so rich that the words were rendered nearly incomprehensible by my uninitiated ears.

"Do you know 'Moonlight Sonata?'" I shouted. He smiled stupidly at me and nodded—his fingers still tapping out some obscure Russian favorite. "'Moonlight Sonata,'" I repeated. He did not speak. He just continued to smile and nod. "Great," I said, as I turned to descend the stairs leading to the bathroom. "You don't understand a word I'm saying. Do you, you old fuck?"

The stairs were steep and went deep. So deep that when I finally reached the bottom, the piano music had dwindled to a dull, distant, melody. I approached the bathroom's entrance and fell against it. The door swung open at a dangerous velocity, and slammed into the long, marble sink—liberating a sliver of long, silver stone that fell solidly down to the urine-soaked floor.

I let the door go free and stumbled toward the nearest urinal. My pant's zipper was barely undone before I loosed a torrent of brown, splashing piss. My back arched, and I began to moan—the sensation of release bordered on orgasmic. When the stream began to die, I clenched my asshole tightly and watched as one last jet of liquid waste splashed into the urinal's shallow bowl.

There was a strange tapping next to me—within the bathroom's only stall. I zipped my pants, and, for the first time since coming down the stairs, I listened. There was not one, but two hushed voices coming from within the small, one-man stall.

"That's a fat line," said one.

"I don't fuck around," said the other.

Then came a loud sucking sound—like a narrow mouthed vacuum inhaling a pile of sand, or cocaine bouncing up a rolled hundred-dollar bill into someone's eager nostril.

I cleared my throat, loudly; much too loud to be anything other than a noise intended to alert and interrupt. Then, I moved toward the stall door and situated my left eye to peer through the gap in the stall's frame.

"You guys having a party in there?" I asked as I pressed my body against the brushed stainless steel.

From behind the door came another vacuuming sound, then an exaggeratedly deep voice asked, "You need a bump?"

"I need five," I laughed. "Can you accommodate me?"

There was a duet of giggles from behind the door. "Do you have the money?" one of the two asked through the gap.

"Yes, I do"

"Are you sure?" asked the other.

"I'm sure," I said as I opened and scanned the contents of my wallet.

"Well then, get your ass in here."

I went into the stall with a newly cashed check in my wallet—five hundred dollars, and a little bit of change. I left with nothing. But luckily, I had money left on my debit card. Enough to pay from my drinks, at least.

I ascended the stairs slowly—careful to take in my environment. I knew, in the logical part of my mind, that the bar was dark, but, to my eyes, it looked bright. Bright, and clean, and pure, and . . .

What is that noise? I wondered. *Music? Piano?* I had not noticed it at first, but now that I had heard it, I could hear nothing else. The melody exploded into my ears with a terrible intensity. I reeled against it, nearly stumbling into the arms of a thin, feminine looking man who was eyeing me suspiciously.

I brandished my most disgusted looking expression at the bastard and screamed, "Don't look at me like that, you fuck! It's fucking loud!" He scowled at me, and I gave him a stiff, one finger wave. "Fucker," I muttered as I walked away.

On my way back to my empty barstool, and the busty blonde, I slowed down for a moment and looked for speakers around the gigantic grand piano. I found none.

But the music is impossibly loud, screamed a voice in my mind. *It couldn't just be coming from the piano, could it?*

"Could it?" I echoed the question aloud.

Kill it, demanded the scared, angry, little boy's voice in my brain—the same voice that began to shout and complain every time I exceeded my limit of drug and drink. Was it my id? My super-ego? The onset of full-blown paranoid schizophrenia? Or, maybe, it was just the same scared, insecure, irrational, little child that hides within the core of all adults?

"Shut up you bastard!" I begged. "Shut up, can't you see that I'm trying to think?" My shouts were lost within the enormously loud, waltzing dirge being played on the piano.

Kill it, the child's voice hissed.

"Shut up. You're not the boss of me, you murderous bastard. I won't kill anything for you. Not again. Not ever." I gave my chest several heavy hits with the meaty side of my fist and momentarily felt winded. "See what you get when you fuck around?" I asked, wheezing. "Try me again. See what happens. I dare you. See what happens." The voice in my head remained silent. It did not dare risk instigating my wrath. Over our many shared years, it had grown smart. It had learned my limits. It had learned to obey.

I approached the pianist, pinched at the air, and began to rotate my fingers—the universal hand signal for: "Turn it down". He looked concerned, almost scared. "Turn it down," I shouted. "Down." He smiled at me nervously. "Down," I repeated in a scream so primal that the action hurt my throat. Still, despite my effort, the word was not audible over the apocalyptic boom of piano keys being struck. "Down. Please. My ears are bleeding." The pianist smiled more enthusiastically. He seemed to finally understand my meaning. "Thank you," I mouthed. But he did not see display of gratitude. He had already returned to his default posture—head down, pleasantly, rhythmically nodding.

I turned, navigated a maze of drunkards, and poured myself down onto my seat. The beautiful, busty blonde was talking to her equally beautiful brunette friend. Playing hard to get, I pulled out my notebook, turned silently away from them, and began to write.

The words on the page were worthless—a meaningless rant about the importance of humanity's existence on the cosmic stage. A thesis based on the idea that our universe is a giant organism and that we, as the only scientifically advanced life form in all of creation, are not only stewards of the cosmos, but, also, its conflicted, depressed, juvenile brain.

In the periphery of my vision, I spotted movement. I turned my head and saw the pianist eyeing me with an enormous grin. *Why?* I wondered. The music was still loud. He had not turned down the volume like I had asked. *Why the fuck is he smiling? Is he trying to pick a fight? Fucker will get his teeth knocked out if he . . .*

The music changed. The frantic notes morphed with an impossible grace. They melted, mixed, and transformed from a menacing, fast-paced carnival song to the somber, soft, slow melody that had been the soundtrack to many of my most enchanted dreams.

"Moonlight Sonata," like I had never previously heard it performed. It was as slow as a sunset but—innumerably—more moving.

I looked down at my disposable Varsity fountain pen and felt a warmth build in my bloated, beer distended belly. A warmth that moved up to my chest, and, finally, settled in my flushed red cheeks. I flipped to a blank page and began to write. Going slowly at first—careful to enjoy the curve of every letter—I wrote this:

Sofia, our story is not unique.
Special? Oh yes. Absolutely special.
But not unique.
Boy meets girl. That is the meaning of life, and it happens every day.

Jack Webb

Humans. We. Us. The multitude. Billions of bipeds constantly beating our feet against the good Earth as we dance around our mates.

An elegant, species wide, whirling waltz. An infinitely complex, and rewarding, exercise.

We dance this dance. We step . . . oh, we step . . . but our dance— yours and mine—is different. Our posture, our style, our tempo—all these things and more—are different. These differences are small, sometimes nearly unnoticeable, But they are there.

When we twirl for example. The way the spinning pulls me away from you, and the way you always pull me back. The way I step on your toes. The way I step on my own toes. The way I stumble. And the way you always manage to keep me on my feet.

The way you so often lead. And the way I happily follow. The way you dip me instead of being dipped. The way you hold me up. The way you keep me from falling. They way I sometimes carry you in my arms when you are tired, and the music refuses to slow.

Like children, who are just learning to stand, we glide and stumble across the dance floor. We wobble loosely and with seemingly no direction. Yet we continue to hold each other, and we quit the dance.

I do not know how we continue, and I do not know why. It seems like we should have fallen out of step with each other a long time ago.

No. I do not know how we continue. But I am thankful that we do.

You have made my life better in ways that I have only just begun to discover.

If we were to end today—if the music stopped—I would cry tears of joy. Not because I would be happy to leave you. No, certainly not.

I would cry because I would be happy to have had you. Together for the rest of our lives, or done tomorrow—it does not matter. I have known you. Whatever happens next is inconsequential. I have already won.

Forever, or just until the end of this song, your dancing partner,

Christopher Scott Christian

"Moonlight Sonata" tapered to a slow end. And with it ended my letter. I dropped the pen and read over what I had written. A vision of Sofia briefly flashed behind my eyes and was quickly replaced by a black resentment that felt very much like hatred.

Why don't we have sex anymore? I wondered. *Am I that disgusting? Why won't she touch me? I know that I have put on some weight. But, I'm not fat. It isn't fair. I look good. It isn't right that . . .*

There was a tap on my shoulder. I looked up at the beauty beside me. Her wet, red lips were stretched into a long, toothy smile. I smiled back, momentarily aware that the teeth glistening at me were at least three shades whiter than my own.

This woman . . . she was beyond attractive. And, more than that, she was far beyond *me*. And I knew it. But, fortunately, I too was far beyond me at the moment. So, feeling ambitious, I decided to go for it.

"What's up, gorgeous?" I asked with a slur. She giggled. Giggled at my cuteness? Maybe. Or was it my cheeky question? Most likely, it was my heavy, drunken lisp that she found amusing. I did not know for sure, but I took it as a good sign.

"You think I'm cute?" I questioned, leaning to her. Again she stretched her luscious lips into a long, lovely smile.

"Maybe," she groaned, with a playful shrug of her slender shoulders.

That was all the approval I required. I stared intently into her eyes—making what I believed to be a seductive expression—and then, mouth first, I lunged.

She fell back against her friend. *No problem,* I thought. *She wasn't expecting such animal intensity. I just caught her off-guard, that's all.*

I lunged again, and she dodged, narrowly avoiding my lips. I lunged a third time. Then a fourth. A fifth.

Missed. Missed. Missed.

I turned away, paid my bill, and left the bar—tapping her chummily on the shoulder as I escaped the awkward scene.

The night went black and the events of the next three hours are missing from my memory. The only hints are a few incomprehensible text messages mentioning Columbus Circle, a fight, wet shoes, and the emotion *fear*, written several times and in all capital letters.

Hours passed and I knew nothing but blackness. Then, all at once, I was back. Like an exposed nerve, I was terribly—painfully—aware.

"Pull over," I begged in a soft, gasping, choking, burping voice. "Please, please, pull over. I'm sick." The person driving the car responds with obvious amusement. Though his words belonged to a language other than my own, the glee in his voice was unmistakable. "Pull over, I'm dying," I belched. "Over . . . dying."

The taxi ground to a slow stop. Impatient, I opened the door and looked out at the rain-wet street slowly passing beneath me.

When the cab finally jerked to a halt, I fell from my seat and hit the ground. Then it came. Release. A powerful stream of chunky, yellow-pink matter tore its way up my esophagus and out from my mouth. Heaving, belching, puking, I tried to climb to my knees and escape the foul puddle that was spreading in every direction. I clawed at the open door, and the worn fabric of the cab's back seat. Finally, the stream of burning fluid stopped, just long enough for my lungs to take a wet, savage breath.

Still holding on to the taxi, every muscle in my body contracted violently. A powerful, primal, survival reflex. My body had been poisoned. I had poisoned it, and, now, it was struggling to stay alive. Pride? Dignity? Such high-minded ideas ceased to exist. All concerns were secondary to the main objective—purge. I would have to deal with my shame later.

A convulsion pushed putrid bile dripping out from the corners of my eyes, streaming from my nose, and rocketing from my mouth. At the opposite end of my body, the situation was even worse.

One more convulsion, and then the evacuation of my digestive system was complete. I could feel the seat of my pants grow hot and heavy. Urine added liquidity to firm diarrhea, and the chunky mixture coated my testicles and dripped slowly down the back of my thighs.

The cabby exited the car and came to examine his filthy fare.

I looked up and was barely able to register the amused grin on his face before another convulsion gripped my body. Burps replaced vomit. Wet, gasping farts replaced shit.

"You're really sick, huh?" He inquired with a chuckle. "Yeah. You're really sick. Maybe you drink too much. Yeah?"

I nodded in agreement and the action triggered another convulsion. When it finally subsided, I felt used-up, thin, and empty—like a spent tube of toothpaste. The only difference being that, instead of Artic Mint, the smells around me were those of alcohol, acid, and ass juice.

I reached for my wallet with one hand and signaled the cabby to stay back with the other. He had already watched me puke . . . I did not want to give him the added satisfaction of discovering my shitty pants.

I fumbled with my wallet as several dry heaves repeatedly punched me in the gut. Finally, I managed to pluck out my emergency credit card—the one with the high credit limit, and even higher interest rate.

The outstretched card trembled between my unsteady fingers. The pitiless driver snatched it from me and returned to the cab.

Here . . . things go black again. Events transpired . . . perhaps mundane . . . perhaps spectacular. I do not know. I do not remember. Where a memory should be, there is nothing but an impenetrable blackness.

And then, in an explosion of disorienting brilliance, I am back.

"Save me, Sofia. Please, I'm dying. I don't know where I am. I'm dying. No, no, I'm not joking. I'm dying. Please. No. Yes. Thank you. Thank you. Hurry. And bring a new pair of pants. Why? I'm dying . . . I'm dying, Sofia. No. Hurry. Pants. No. Please, please Sofia. Save me. No. I don't *know* where I am. I'm on the sidewalk. I'm lying on the sidewalk. I don't know where I am . . . I'm lying in a puddle. I'm going to drown," I cried. "Save me. Please. I can't see the sign. It's blurry. Everything is blurry. Sofia, please save me." I began to sob uncontrollably. "I . . . I . . . I shit my pants. I shit my pants. I shit . . . shit. Jesus, I'm dying. Save me, Sofia. Save . . . okay . . . okay . . . okay. I'll send you a picture."

I dropped the phone from my ear and fumbled to press the "End" button. Then I brought the phone close to my face and squinted at the glowing screen. After several seconds of searching, I found the camera application. I aimed the lens at the street sign overhead and captured an image. Some few taps later and the picture was sent. Gone. Just like my consciousness.

This time the break in my memory is long. How long? I do not care to know. I do not care to know.

The hand on my shoulder is dry, soft, and warm. Eyes still closed from my trip to oblivion, I leaned into its tender touch.

Slowly, I began to wake from my dreamless, alcohol-induced coma. It was still nighttime, but the world looked bright to my swollen, bloodshot eyes. Above me hovered an angel. Her wings were wide and white. Her skin was a chalky brown. And her long, curly, almond hair was cascaded delicately down the left side of her delicate angel's face.

The seraph's hand pulled away from my shoulder and reached around to a fluffy, white cloud floating at her back. From it she extracted a pair of faded brown Dockers. Thirty-six by thirty-four; they were my size.

She said something, but she was speaking angel, and I had never gotten around to learning that language. To complicate things more, it appeared as if she did not know English.

When I tried to tell her that I did not understand, she simply shook her head sympathetically and smiled a confused, pitying smile. Desperate to communicate, I looked up into her eyes and was nearly blinded by the light emanating from her halo.

The angel said something, in her divine singsong language, and helped me to my feet. I stumbled. *Of course I stumbled.* But she caught me. She held me up.

I began to walk—eyes closed, and striding like a blind man. I let the angel lead me.

In her arms, I staggered down a curb, tripped up a curb, and made my way to ground that felt soft and pliable beneath my bare feet.

The angel's arms let me go, and I fell to the Earth's soft, squishing surface. The smell of the ground pressed against my nose was unmistakable. Grass. A wet, soft, clean, wonderful bed of grass. The perfect bed for a quick nap.

Blackness. Only this time, the segment of missing memory is short.

A tugging, jerking sensation woke me. Someone was trying to pull off my pants.

"Sofia," I whined. "Help me. I'm dying."

Then returns the blackness. Blackness. Blackness.

"What?" I choked. "What are you? What are you doing?" I felt a thick, coarse fabric wipe my ass. It was painful. I tried to cry out—to beg for relief—but I could not. Something cold and hard caught itself on the tissue-paper flesh of my alcoholic's asshole, and I could feel something rip. I tried to cry out, but the blackness reclaimed me instead.

When I came back to me, I was flying. Soaring. Feeling the speed, but not the wind. Acceleration. Deceleration. Acceleration. Deceleration. Full stop. Acceleration. A sudden jolt followed by a violent bump. Deceleration.

I heard a loud honk from a car's horn. The sound was huge. "Traffic in heaven," I chuckled.

A voice came then. The angel? No. It was a familiar voice—intimately familiar. What was it saying? What?

Was it "I wish you wouldn't drink so often"? Was it "You have to stop doing this to me"? Was it "I love you, but I can't keep doing this"?

Was it all of these things.

Was it all of these things, and more?

Probably.

What sort of a man am I that even angels struggle to love me?

Chapter 13

I approached the guy casually, nodded, and asked, "Dude, can I get a dub?" He turned his head to meet me, and I watched as his eyes began to scream in fear. He obviously did not like strangers. "A dub?" I repeated.

His lips clenched into a tight pucker that—and, I think this can be stated fairly—looked exactly like a German Shepherd's shitty asshole. In response, I stretched my own mouth into what—I hope—looked like a confused and questioning frown. In response to my response, he simply shook his head, crossed his arms, and looked off at some unknowable, and unknowably smug distance—of which it was his exclusive pleasure to gleam.

"Dude, come on, I live right across the street." I pointed to my building, and my apartment's approximate location within it. "I buy from you guys all the time." The asshole on his face began to relax its tight sphincter-like muscle, and I began to feel hope build explosively in my chest. The sensation made me giddy, excited, and scared. So, I did what it is that I do when I become scared. I started humiliating and debasing myself for cheap laughs, and to give the impression that I was not a threat.

"It's because I'm white . . . isn't it?" The guy continued looking off—unfazed by the unimpressive joke. But the youngest member of his crew was cracking. I could see it. The corner of his mouth; it was practically vibrating. "Listen, man, don't let these beautiful, baby blue eyes fool you. I've smoked forests of trees. And, right now, I am just trying to pack my bowl. Dude, my stomach hurts. Don't leave me hanging. I need some weed, dude. My track . . ." I motioned to my beer belly. "I'm bloated as fuck, dude. Help me out." No one moved—except me. I clutched my gut, playfully, and began to whip it around at them. "Come on." Still nothing. It was becoming obvious to me that I had struck out.

"Fuck you guys," I exclaimed. "That's some racist shit, let me tell you." Still, no one moved. But, the kid in the back, the one with the sense of humor, was not smiling anymore. He looked pissed. Pissed at the dude, just as I was pissed at him. "Fuck it. If you guys decide to quit being dicks, I'll be over on my stoop." Again, I pointed to my building, just in case any of them had forgotten. "I'mma wait for my normal guy over there."

With that, I turned, slowly walked to the corner, crossed the road, walked to my building, stood on my stoop, and stared at them. If Sofia could have seen me then, she would have said that I was doing my "Crazy Whiteman" impression. I always found that funny. She always had such an optimistic view of the world, and of me. She saw impressions, where I saw a complete lack of perspective and honest, violent, lunatic rage.

I stared at them; and stared; and stared; and stared. Until, dear God, finally, reason returned to me, and I began to—ever, so slowly—regain my sanity.

Murder? No. That no longer seemed reasonable. So, instead of confronting the group, and demanding they sell me my damned medicine—lest I beat them *all* to death—I plucked my phone from my pocket and began to read the news.

The North Korean government is so damned needy, I thought. *What we need to do is drop shrooms in their fucking water. Give those fuckers some damned social skills. Shrink their egos enough for them to finally mature enough to play with the rest of the kids in class.*

"Yo," said a young, friendly voice in front of me. "Sorry, about Tyler, he's new. This is his first day."

"Not a big deal. Sorry that I got pissed. I'm hung-over as fuck." I handed him the money, and he handed me my medicine. "Thanks a lot, dude. Have a good day."

"You too," he said, and then reapplied the hood of his hoody to his neatly groomed head.

Chapter 14

Excerpt from writing journal.
Location: PaperClips break room
Date: Unknown
Time: Approx. 10:00am
Author: Christopher Christian

Sitting here at work. I can't help but wonder if this is it? Can I even do better? I went to school and got a degree. A big, smelly, expensive Bachelor's.

Bachelor's in Visual Arts. Visual Arts? I hate visual art. I'm all about the verbal . . . oral arts. Words.

After I graduated I realized I was really in love with the written word.

The written word . . .

What the hell? What do I know about the written word? I didn't learn to read until I was ten years old. I didn't really learn to write until I was fifteen . . .

So, again . . . is this it? I have a degree in something I hate, and I like to do something in which I am completely unqualified. I'm a lifetime behind.

Writers are a competitive breed . . . and me? I couldn't spell until . . . well . . . I still misspell with alarming regularity.

Punctuation? Jesus; the semicolon is still a mystery to me. Someone tried to describe it to me as a weak period? Blah.

Am I kidding myself? Do I really think I have what it takes? Not just to be a writer, but anything at all? I'm white trash. A stupid country bumpkin. I'm from New York, sure. But the green part of the state, where cows roam, and Nazi wannabes hate. Hate and play violent games with people of color and those they deem as "Fags."

I don't brush as often as I should, I eat shit, I'm rash, hostile, self-indulgent, and have a wildly overblown sense of self worth. In truth, I am beginning to suspect that any amount of ego—even a small amount—would be . . . overblown.

I am flaws all over.

I'm a writer? I'm nothing. Just another stupid boy trying to pass as a man. Just another trashy Christian.

Should I be happy? After all I am working in the city. Andy Warhol said something like: "Success is a job in New York City."

I live in the city. I have a job. I am successful. Right? By his definition I am.

Ugh. Should I burn this notebook? Will these words

mean anything? Do they mean anything? Am I actually writing? Could this even be considered writing?

Am I writing a book or just indulging myself? Is this stack of crumpled, dirty paper my future or am I just masturbating?

"Chris?" The store manager sounded angry. "Clock back in from break. I need to talk to you."

"Okay. One second."

"No. Not in one second. Now."

Ah, the sweet taste of success.

I could feel the gears grinding in my cheeks. The rusty pegs creaked as they pulled a smile across my face.

The mouth yelling at me could have been an advertisement against smoking cigarettes.

He pointed a fat, dirty finger at me and said, "I asked you to explain it again."

His breath whistled around and through the stubby brown remnants of his teeth. It burned my nose and made the back of my tongue itch. Not wanting him to see the disgust that must have been present on my face, I broke eye contact and looked down at his shirt.

The shirt was blue, cotton, button-down, and of much higher quality than mine. On his left sleeve was an oval patch that said manager.

My breath was slow and shaky. I was trying not to smell.

Hesitantly, I began to speak. "Umm." The word

vibrated painfully through my thinly drawn and toothy smile. "The customer said she was a tourist from Brazil—here for the weekend. I assumed . . . " *Fuck. Wrong word.* "I assumed . . . wrongly; I realize that now . . . that she wouldn't have a rewards card."

He sucked air, and then spit it out of the corner of his mouth. The action made a sharp tsk-tsk sound. Then he did it again but with emphasis, "Tissffk. Tissffk."

"Seems to be a lot of that happening around here. People *assuming.* Thinking they know what is best. What is best for the customers. What is best for business. Making decisions without consulting management. Yes. You *should* try to address that. Assuming is definitely something *you* need to work on."

My smile thinned even more.

"What else did you do wrong?" he asked as he looked down and wrote, "makes assumptions" in bright red on the Worker Evaluation Sheet.

"I . . . I umm."

I honestly can't think of anything. It could be any-thing. Did their receipt have a survey? Did I remember to tell them that if they filled it out they would have a chance to win a five-thousand-dollar gift card? Did I up sell—sell them the laser rather than the standard paper?

Oh shit, it was the greeting, wasn't it? I got the script wrong. I asked, "Can I help you find anything?" Instead of the more leading, "What can I help you find today?"

Impatient, he volunteered the answer. "The pens."

Of course.

"You forgot to try and sell her the pen of the

month. You know we are trailing in pen sales. I know you know, because during our last rally meeting I made it a point to emphasize how important it is to sell the pens."

Fuck. The pens . . . how? Oh, how could I have forgotten about the pens?

"Yes. I remember, Eric. It slipped my mind. Sorry, it will not happen again." The smile weighed heavily on my face.

Trying to end on a high note, Eric said, "Hey, listen. On the plus side. You sure were *very* nice. Can't nobody complain about that. Very nice and very engaging."

I screamed in my head: *Engaging? Fuck off. Don't patronize me. I don't need this. I have a degree, you son of a bitch. What's the most you've managed to get? A GED? Did you even get that? I would not be surprised if you didn't even graduate middle school. Aaahh.*

"Thank you, Eric. That means a lot to me. I really try to get to know the customer." The words slid like acid off my tongue. Each syllable burned. I could not care less for the customers. It was all I could do not to spit in their faces and punch them in their guts.

"Kudos, kid. That's all for now." His fist extended toward me. He was looking for a fist bump; casual, impersonal, and awkward. I met his fist and winced as his long, sharp knuckles buried themselves between mine. They hit a nerve.

Ouch.

He walked away and I could see him scribble, "Nice to customers" on the Worker Evaluation Sheet. I wanted to quit. But then I thought about Andy Warhol. This *was* success.

I guess I will stay.

A voice, frantic and angry, shouted over the PA system, "Chris, will you *please* come to the front for a customer consultation?"

From my position in back I could see that there was a crowd developing around the register. People were mashing against each other. I could feel their body heat.

I hate this place.

I took a deep breath and charged into the crowd like a fireman into a burning building—confident, despite the flames.

My smile was wide.

Chapter 15

The double-doors sprang open and Cooper strode into the store. He was dressed in a red button-down shirt, suit vest and jeans; all wrinkled.

"You're late," I laughed.

"Fuck it. I'm sick," he said as he brushed up next to me and clocked in at the register. I smelled beer on his clothes and on his breath.

Maria chirped from behind one of the isles, "Cooper. You're late."

We looked up and around but neither of us could see her. Maria was short and the aisles—slightly taller than she—hid her effortlessly.

Cooper cleared his throat coarsely. "I'm sick. Jesus.

I almost didn't make it in at all," he said with his usual thick southern accent. He forced a cough but did not bother to cover his mouth or play the role of someone who was coughing. He simply made the noise. He sounded convincing. Hot breath and the smell of beer surrounded me.

I followed Cooper back to the break room and said, "Damn, man. You didn't bring your clothes? How are you going to work?"

"I never take my uniform home." He said this with such conviction that I believed him.

"How do you clean them?"

"Clean them? Shit." He smiled and shook his head.

"You've been working here for how long? And you've never cleaned your uniform?" I asked.

"Listen. It's not like we do hard work here. I never get dirty. Fuck, boy. Why waste the water?" He jumped up and pulled wrinkled blue and black fabric from between boxes on the second to top shelf above the break room table.

Watching him fumble with the fabric, I said, "I just wear my uniform to work. It is easier than getting changed."

He backed into the break room corner nearest the microwave; it was a notorious camera blind spot.

He pulled his pants down but they caught on his boots. He twisted and tugged at them but they were stubborn. Finally they gave, and he almost fell; I almost laughed.

He looked at me disapprovingly and said, "I

wouldn't be caught dead in public wearing this. Are you kidding me? This clown suit? It's enough to have to work at PaperClips. I don't want to go around advertising it."

"Well at least you *are* employed. And, at least you're not working at McDonald's. You know?" He did not reply to my question. Not the slightest bit of acknowledgment. It was as if he had not heard me.

All at once, in one fluid motion, he pulled off his vest, button-down, and undershirt. Then Cooper hurled them up onto the shelf.

I continued, "Andy Warhol said, 'Success is a job in New York City.'"

Cooper shook his head and said, "Yeah . . . well I don't know who Andy Warhol is, but I think he sounds like a stupid sonofabitch."

Yeah, I think so too.

Chapter 16

The clock read 2:45pm.

I should have been out of work fifteen minutes ago.

"Yes, ma'am, we do print photographs. If you could just step over to the consulting table Maria will help you." *As soon as she finishes spending five hours holding that man's hand as he gets thirty-six cents worth of black-and-white prints.*

It had been slow since the lunch rush, yet Maria had still managed to develop a line. She heard me tell the woman to step to the consulting table and looked at me with disbelief. She seemed astonished that I could not see how busy she was.

Frantic, she said, "Will you wait a moment, sir?" The gentlemen she was working with nodded. He clearly did not care. He seemed to have mastered the print button and needed little help from her.

Maria shuffled quickly to a black office phone, picked up the receiver and pressed a large green button. A red light kicked on next to the button and she spoke into the microphone. "Can I please have a consultant to the consulting table?" Her voice sounded accusatory. It was as if she meant to say, "Why is there *not* another consultant at the consulting table?"

I turned around and saw Cooper walking to the front. He was sweating. His eyes were bloodshot. And, though I could not see it, I was sure that he was shaking.

He was drunk when he came into work. He was drunk and the slow advance of sobriety had made him sick. His pale cheeks said that he was in danger of barfing.

The door to the store opened slowly. The person who entered had the hood of a sweater pulled up, exposing only her chin.

Being a good little pawn, I said, "Welcome to PaperClips. What can I help you find today?"

She pulled down her hood. It was Tiffany, the service expert.

Tiffany was the *expert* in charge of sales; an expert at locating pens, paper, and ink. "Oh yes. Aisle two is where we keep the Wite-Out. It is next to the markers. What's that? Thank you? Of course. No problem. That's why I am the service expert."

I greeted her. With a large, goofy smile, I exclaimed, "Tiffany! How are you?"

Finally, I can leave, I thought.

Weary, Tiffany said, "Hey, Chris. Hey, Maria."

Maria did not respond. She was busy frantically doing nothing.

Tiffany clocked in at the register next to me and I clocked out. I followed her to the break room. When we got to our destination, she positioned herself against the coat hangers. She was in my way . . . keeping me from my sweater and, by extension, my exit.

Move, I thought, but said nothing.

She turned to face the wall and pulled the hoodie off, over her head. She was wearing a thin-strapped tank top and her upper back was visible. The skin there was brown, bare, and smooth. No bra. She turned again, but in my direction.

The fabric of her tank top was white cotton. I could see her dark nipples through the thin fabric. She did not know or she did not care. Regardless, I had trouble looking away.

Trying to break the spell I asked, "Damn, where is my book?"

Tiffany responded, "Think I put my purse on it."

"Oh yeah. Look at that. You did," I said and began to chuckle awkwardly. My heart was beating quickly and I could feel my cheeks growing warm. Blood vessels, all over my body, were dilating . . . swelling with blood. I felt like an overripe tomato.

She extended a hand toward her bag and tried to snap her fingers but her long, neon pink, plastic nails undermined her intentions. Finally, she asked, "Pass it to me?"

"Sure." I picked up the large leather purse and handed it to her. Surprised by the bag's weight, I said, "Wow. Heavy."

"You ain't lying. I keep my life in my purse." She undid the purse's thick copper latch, dug in up to her elbow and pulled out black pants and a blue shirt.

Her jeans were skintight. She had no problem pulling her stretchy black work pants over them. Then, she pulled her already buttoned button-down over her head and tucked it into her pants.

"You wear pants . . . under your work pants?" I asked.

"Yeah. Always have."

She spoke with such a strong urban accent that—to my upstate adapted ears at least—her "Always have." sounded more like "Alwaves Ave." and I could not help but to admire her city girl's mouth.

"So . . . a little late?" I asked.

"Yeah. I am mad hungover. Almost didn't come in."

I could see Cooper out on the floor. He was impatiently consulting the woman I had directed to Maria. In the distance I could hear Cooper say, "Ma'am, listen. No one lied to you. We are totally capable of printing your pictures. All I am trying to tell you is that we specialize in printing documents. I can print your pictures on glossy photo paper. That's no problem. But, we only print on standard letter sized paper. If you want them four by six . . . fine. That we can do. I can print three to a page. I can do that for you no problem. You are just going to have to cut them out yourself."

"Hungover? It happens," I said.

I looked at the clock on the microwave and thought, *I'm just glad that I can get the fuck out of here.*

She palmed her breasts and adjusted them in her shirt. I tried not to stare and failed. She caught my gaze and I felt my cheeks flush even more.

Intense embarrassment filled me. Not knowing what to do, I attempted to advance the conversation. Nervously, I asked, "Crazy night last night?"

"Yeah. I was at the bar and my ex showed up." She shook her head regretfully and then continued, "She started shit and we got in a fight. I punched her in the face and scratched her forehead." I looked at her with surprise, but said nothing. "She kicked me in the shin. I have a bruise." She pulled up both layers of pants and showed me a blue-green-black knot on her leg.

Honestly surprised, I said, "Ouch."

"Yeah. I feel bad though. I fucked her up. I think the cuts on her forehead are gunna scar." She clicked her long nails together and held them up for me to see. "I had skin in my nails. Didn't realize until I got home."

The conversation paused as I tried to absorb all the information. After a moment, I asked, "You said, she . . . as in girlfriend?"

"Yeah. You don't know? I'm a lesbian."

How could I know? This is our first real conversation, I thought.

"No, I didn't know. But . . . I thought you had a boyfriend."

"Oh, I don't call him my boyfriend."

Confused, I asked, "But you're still with him . . . right? So, you're not a lesbian. You're bi."

I read shame on her face but could not understand why. She looked at the ground and said, "Yeah . . . I guess. That is new, though. He is the first guy I have ever been with."

"Well, congratulations," I said and smiled sincerely. I *was* sincere. She was comfortable with herself. She was comfortable with her sexuality. That took a lot. That took a lot of confidence. I respected that. I was attracted to that.

I reached around her and grabbed my sweater. She moved toward me at the same time and my arm slid along under her breasts.

She did not move. She did not so much as flinch. Her breasts dragged along my arm and trailed my hand as I pulled the sweater to my chest.

Seemingly unaware that we just went to second base, Tiffany leaned down and tucked her jeans into her socks.

My thoughts raced. *An accident. It doesn't mean anything. Calm down. Don't get any ideas. But . . . she had to have felt it. I mean . . . how could she not. Jesus. What is this?* I was in awe.

Slowly, and with palpable trepidation, I began to speak. "Tiffany . . . " She looked up and smiled. Still incredibly uneasy, I continued, "I'll see you later, huh? Have fun tonight."

Her smile melted to expose a look of utter disappointment.

Struggling to make sense of what was going on I thought, *I don't understand. I'm so fucking confused. What is this? What is happening?*

"Yeah. I'll try," she said before looking back down at her pants.

"Have fun with Maria," I joked.

Tiffany rolled her eyes and said, "Pft. Yeah, I know. She should be gone by now. She will probably stay until eight. She is milking that overtime."

"Overtime?" I asked.

"Yeah, why else do you think she would keep staying so late?"

I shrugged my shoulders and said, "I dunno. Maybe she hates to go home."

We both laughed.

Chapter 17

I unlocked my door and eased my way into our apartment. The air was stale but comforting. It smelled like me mixed with her. I had not seen her in a month—my phantom bed partner. Not since that day at the restaurant.

At night, she would sneak in while I was asleep. When I left in the morning, my eyes were often so thick with dreams and crust that I could scarcely make out her shape in our bed.

Leaving for work I would shout, "Have a good day." In reply she would shuffle between the sheets.

I sniffed the air and closed the door to our apartment. I was walking to the fridge to grab a beer when my phone chirped and vibrated in my pocket. The text read,

"You piece of shit. You left without me." It was Cooper. We normally took the train together, but recently I had been avoiding him.

He scared me. The fear was not so much of Cooper as it was of the trouble he might cause while I was around him. Trouble I would have liked to avoid.

The previous week someone was "looking at him" on the train.

"Yo . . . I think that guy wants to kiss me." Cooper's voice was sharp and its tone unexpectedly severe. The man sitting across from us appeared to be in his fifties. He had a medium length gray and white beard. On his nose rested thick lenses in a thin silver frame. He was dressed fashionably in a suit and tie.

The lenses he wore made it hard for me to determine the object of his gaze. I could not tell if he was looking at Cooper, or the advertisement above Cooper's head. Either way his look did not seem hostile.

Cooper continued, "He thinks just because he's black that he's better then me." I was astonished. I was amazed. I was suddenly and completely uncomfortable. I did not know what to say. I said nothing.

"He thinks I am scared of him. He thinks I won't start something. He thinks I won't start something because I'm white. He thinks I'm soft."

Quietly, I said, "No. I think he is just looking at the sign above your head."

"No . . . what . . . are you blind? He is staring right at me. Fuck, the nerve of this guy." Cooper shook his head, gritted his teeth, and continued, "What? Am I just supposed sit here and take this shit? I don't deserve this. Where I come from people respect each other enough to give'em their space. We don't stare or point. Them's the rules. Common fucking courtesy." His words grew loud and I became aware that though he was talking to me, he was speaking for the benefit of the stranger. "It's common fucking courtesy. Staring is rude. And . . . where I come from, liable to get someone shot." He was scowling at the man. He had the focus of a dog. Waiting anxiously for the command to attack: he was drooling for an excuse to bite.

I looked at him and said, "Listen, you are in the city now. People stare here. It happens. You just have to ignore them. You can't fight everyone who stares at you." I had been reading a book, which was still lying open on my lap, and one of its lines was still fresh in my mind. I paraphrased it here. "If you do try to fight everyone . . ." I dropped my voice an octave, put on my best country accent, and quoted, "You'll be busier then a one legged man in an ass kicking contest." I thought it was funny. He did not.

He offered a rebuttal and an impression of his own. "Ooh. Well I don't know. I um. I have far too much paperwork to do. I don't think I have the time to fight. Besides . . . umm . . . my wife . . . why, my wife would kill me if I got my new shirt and tie dirty." His words were a caricature of a White Anglo Saxon Protestant. "And, um, besides, everyone knows those black folks are just so much stronger than us whites. They used to be warriors, you know? Back before those moral-less b . . . ba ba ba . . . butt-holes went down there and forced them into slavery." He tugged at imaginary suspenders and I felt my face flush.

"Excuse my French. I just get so gosh darn angry when I think of all the injustices that they had to endure. Darn it. It wasn't right." The train stopped and the door opened. The man across from us, at whom I had been looking apologetically since Cooper began his tirade, rose and made for the door.

The stranger's expression was unchanged from when I first became aware of him and when he passed I realized he was wearing small, in-ear headphones. The cords hanging from the headphones were thin and attached to a music player he was holding in his hand. I felt a rush of relief. The poor guy did not deserve to hear this. No one did. As the man passed Cooper began blowing him wet kisses. The man left, seemingly unaware.

Cooper looked at me and said, "Fuck. Can you believe that guy? Staring like that?" I picked up my book and began to read. Cooper continued speaking despite my unwillingness to reply. "Sorry about that. It just really fucking upsets me. To be stared at like that really makes me uncomfortable. People in the city have this *idea* about white people. The media . . . rap music. They don't help."

I continued to read. Cooper continued to rant. "I tell you, man. There is a situation brewing. If the media keeps portraying whites as a soft people . . . people who just turn the other cheek . . . " He shook his head. "That's just not how it is. That's not the reality. Know whaddaimean? White people are crazy. We war all of the time. That is what we do. We fight. We are fighters. You know?" I kept reading. "It's dangerous is all I am saying. The more people say that white people are weak, the more white people become afraid that people think they are weak. The more white people worry about protecting themselves and their families. The more white people overcompensate. The more white people buy guns."

He suddenly looked tired. Like someone reciting the same old speech to the same non-listening crowd.

Cooper lowered his voice to a civilized volume and said, "Someone is going to step up to a white person looking to push them around. They are going to think it's safe. 'Im'ma push this white guy's buttons. It's no big deal. They are just a bunch of pussies.'" Something like sadness painted his face and he shook his head slowly. "I pity them. Like getting into a cage with a tiger."

Quietly, I said, "You're fucking crazy. You know that?" I spoke but did not look up from my book. People were staring and I did not want them to know that I was with Cooper. I wanted them to think that he was talking to himself. What I really wanted to say was: "Shut up, you fool! You are going to get us killed." But, I was too afraid that this would spark another tirade.

"Don't give me that shit. You know as well as I do that it's true. Ain't anybody going to be better off if public opinion is that white people are victims waiting to be victimized." He paused. The look on his face said that he suddenly realized how crazy he must sound. He looked like a man who had just told a deadly secret. "I'm not racist. Fuck, my uncle is a black man. I've had black friends all my life." I nodded at this but did not speak. I was still pretending not to know him. "I just think it's shitty that I am being categorized like that is all. It's not right. I am more than just my skin color. You know my family came to America after slavery ended? No one in my family has ever owned a slave. I'm just sick to death of people looking at me and thinking shit. I'm white so I must have been a slave owner? I'm white so I must have a white-collar job? I must be successful? I must have money? I must be a pushover? Horseshit."

The train stopped and I got up to leave. He followed close behind. We exited the train station and walked together down a busy street.

Cooper matched my stride and said, "You know . . . I was raised poor-white-trash. My momma was on welfare all my life. Still is. My daddy left when I was just a baby. I met him once and asked him for money to buy a car. I was sixteen and figured he owed me, seeing as how he never got me anything my entire life, and never paid child support. You know what that sonofabitch told me? He told me I should drop out of school and get a *real* job like him. Do construction." I tried to read as we walked. I tried to ignore the lunatic at my side. Regretfully, I could not. I put the book into my pocket and remained silent. "He was living out of a van when I met him. He had been living out of vans and driving all over the country ever since he left my mother. It was his way of staying out of prison when the collection man came knocking."

We passed a post office drop-box and Cooper slapped it. The blue box rang like a bell and people everywhere turned to look at us. Seemingly unaware of the attention he was receiving, Cooper continued speaking. "I wore the same clothes for an entire school year once. People laughed and picked fun, and then I beat their ass. I've always been a tough kid. Not because I wanted to be . . . because I had to be." He cleared his throat and rubbed his eyes. "When I turned eighteen I finally left that Georgia shithole. I went to college in upstate New York. Got a degree and moved my ass to the city. I haven't looked back."

I could see the corner of 207th street and Sherman Ave. Soon he would go left and I would go right. The anticipation was killing me. The whole event had put me on edge.

Sensing that we would soon part ways, Cooper attempted to conclude his tirade. "I'm not racist. Really, I ain't. I think we are *all* humans." I looked at him suspiciously. "I'm poor-white-trash. Born and raised. I am no more that clean, well-dressed, soft spoken, socially conscious, white man on TV than I am a black man. That's all. That's all I'm trying to say." His head hung and he looked tired. "I'm not racist I really ain't. I just say shit. My mouth has always gotten me in trouble. When I get angry I say the worst things that I can think. I just run off at the mouth. I fish for whatever will start a fight. I know . . . it's crazy." I nodded, a healthy nod, in agreement.

He kicked at a rock on the sidewalk and missed it. That act—that simple gesture—humanized him. It was such a small thing; a trivial thing. Missing that rock . . . the effort of the swing and his tremendous lack of aim humanized him. And, through this most innocuous of windows, I saw the man behind the crazy. It *was* a man; not a monster. And, that man looked a lot like me.

Head still hung, Cooper continued, "Shit like what I said on the train? That wild and crazy person I turned into? That guy fits well with the people who raised me. All them back down in the country . . . trailer-park folk . . . they would have been proud of me back there. Only problem is . . . that ain't me. That's only me when I am mad."

I could not wait to end this conversation. *Why in the hell are we walking so slowly? I'll kill this bastard. I swear I will.*

Oblivious to my thoughts, Cooper continued, "I only met my father for a day, but I can tell you this . . . when I get hot under the collar, I sound just like him. It scares me. I lose control. That's why I left. I needed a fresh start. Seems like I fought or burned everyone I had ever known. It was time to start over."

I can't take this shit anymore.

I began to palm at my face in anger and said, "Old habits, huh?"

Surprised, Cooper asked, "What?"

"Listen. I know what you are going through. I really do. But . . ." I stopped walking. "Fuck, man. This is the city. You are going to have to walk away. Especially if you are walking with me. I don't want to get killed, dammit. You think that you are crazy? There are millions of people in the city, and at any given moment most of them are on the street or in the subway. Eventually, you are bound to find someone crazier. You do not need to go looking. Trust me. Jesus, they will find *you*. Trust me. They always do. And, if you do not ignore them, or at the least look away

. . . they are going to stab you with a rusty fucking knife."

"Yeah?" He was looking at me. There was anger there.

"Yeah," I said. I stared into his eyes and stepped closer. I could feel his breath on my face. I tensed and prepared for a fight. None came. After a moment—once I was sure we would not come to blows—I unclenched my fists, patted him on the shoulder, and said, "Look, I have got to get home. I need a beer."

I could feel him staring at me as I left. Hungry eyes. He wanted more. He wanted sympathy. I was unwilling to give it.

Fuck him.

"You piece of shit. You left without me." I reread the message, turned my phone off, and went to the kitchen.

On the fridge, under a magnet, was a note that read:

They had a special on Saranac at the grocery store. I know you like that beer so I bought a six-pack. It is in the fridge. Leave me some. I'm going to be home late. Don't worry about making me dinner. I'll get something on my way home. Love, Sofia.

I grabbed three beers, a bottle opener, and got into the shower.

Chapter 18

"Listen up." Eric, my manager, was at work earlier than usual and he sounded uncharacteristically jolly. Clapping his hands he said, "Listen up, people. Come on. Form a circle. Come on . . . hurry up and form a circle." If he repeated himself less, the smell of cigarette breath in the air might have been easier to ignore. "Hurry up, I said. Hurry up. This announcement will only take a minute."

I looked around and realized who was missing. Maria was still standing at one of the computer stations. She spoke, but her words—blocked behind the monitor—sounded distant. "One second. Just let me send this poster to print." We had no choice but to wait.

Eric reached into his breast pocket and pulled out a

small tube. With one hand he unscrewed the cap. His movements appeared practiced.

A brown fluid squeezed out onto the dry skin of his forefinger and he turned to his left—away from the group.

Unfortunately, I was slightly behind him and to his immediate left. When he opened his mouth I was given an unprecedented, unobstructed, and unwanted view of his rotting maw. His eyes were closed and he could not see me staring. I could not stop staring.

The long, callused index finger traveled far. It was a world of hairy meat and brown stones. The tongue moved and a white spot was revealed. The finger rubbed the brown goo into the ulcer and I could finally look away.

"I am all yours," Maria announced as she joined the group.

Eric smiled and said, "We are going to be making some changes. Maria, you will now be closing. Tiffany, you will now be opening. The hours are out of control, people. This was actually the idea of the district manager himself. He thinks that this little switch will fix our hours problem. I am not so sure I agree." Eric licked his lips and played with the buttons of his shirt. The buttons were tight from the tension of the fabric stretched over his abundant midsection. He tried to pull at them but they did not move.

"I'm not sure it will fix anything," he said, staring at Maria as she left the circle.

"Hi," she said cheerfully. "What can I help you find today?" A customer was at the register and she was off to help them. She did not seem to realize that this meeting was because of her.

Eric's expression changed from one of astonishment to one of anger and he pointed to Tiffany and asked, "Do you know what happens when we go over on the hours?"

"You get written up?" Her response was quick. She knew the answer. Something in their body language—their familiarity—gave me the distinct impression that they had this discussion previously and most likely in private.

"That's right. I get written up. I am the most writ-ten-up manager in the district. I get written up just about every week. Because? That's right. You guessed it. Just about every week we go over on hours." Tiffany nodded and gave him a "go-on" look. After several wheezy breaths, Eric continued, "I have a set number of hours to distribute every week. Those are all the hours our budget allows for me to give. That means, that if we go over on hours we go over on budget, and going over on budget is bad, especially in the eyes of corporate. We are supposed to be making money. Not costing money." He glared out onto the sales floor, at the back of Maria's head. She was alone, standing at a computer. Eric continued, "Every week I have to go down to the district manager's office. He sits me down and gives me the same tired speech about hours and budget. He's sick of explaining it. And, you know what? I'm sick of hearing it. It isn't fun. I don't enjoy it. And I definitely don't like being written up every week." He smiled. I wished he had not. It was a terrible view. I was amazed and terrified that anyone could live with a mouth like that. "Listen, guys. I'm sick of getting written up. Please can we just clock in and out when we are supposed to?"

With as sincere a smile as I could fake, I said, "Sure,

boss."

Eric nodded and said, "I am going to post a new schedule tonight. Chris, you will not be here when I do, so let me just tell you now that your schedule remains the same. Tomorrow morning it will be you, Tiffany, and Cooper opening."

Tiffany looked at me and our eyes met.

"Sweet," I said, not knowing what to say.

The circle dissipated. Tiffany, Eric, and I lingered awkwardly. Trying not to stare into her eyes, I asked, "So, Tiffany, are you excited about working the morning shift?"

"I'm not looking forward to waking up early," she replied.

I rolled my eyes sarcastically and said, "Come on. It is not that bad. I prefer the morning shift. The night shift sucks. You sleep in until noon, come to work, and stay until after the sun sets. Then . . . rinse and repeat. You waste your entire day—every day. The morning shift? I come in before the sun rises, and leave work before I would have even woken up if it was my day off. I have the whole afternoon to be productive. It's almost like not having a job at all." She smiled and I smiled back. Her smile was warm and mine was real.

Eric, in his usual brand of inappropriate humor, said, "You better be careful, Tiffany. Chris will turn you straight." Tiffany blushed and so did I.

I passed Maria as I left work. A line had formed behind the customer she was working with. Five people breathed heavily and fidgeted while waiting for Maria's attention. One of them looked at me and I zipped up my hooded sweater to hide my blue shirt.

Maria did not respond to my goodbye. I was not sure if she heard me. The look on her face was one of serious concentration.

Outside, the air was cool. A strong wind from the south carried the smell of the Atlantic up Broadway. A cool gust engulfed me and I breathed deep.

"Chris."

Fuck.

It was Cooper. "Chris. Wait up."

I should have run away from work. Instead, like a fool, I stopped in front of the store and decided to savor the moment.

"You got out of there quick," he said, rounding me to make eye contact.

"Yeah. I didn't want to stick around more than I had to. Listen, man . . . I can't take the train with you today."

"Why's that?" he asked.

Think. You started this lie, now you've got to finish it. Make it good. This southern fool can smell a lie. Damned if he can't.

Struggling to think of a convincing excuse, I spoke slowly. "Yeah. I know. It sucks. I want to go home, believe me. But . . . my girlfriend is working in the area today and she wants to meet for lunch. I can't stand the old lady up.

You know how it is." I knew he did not. I doubted if he ever felt an obligation to anyone but himself.

Selfish swine.

Visibly disappointed, he said, "Yeah. I guess you shouldn't leave her waiting."

"Yeah. Well. I'll see you tomorrow, Cooper. Try not to kill anyone," I joked. He considered what I had said and smiled tentatively. I pointed over my shoulder with my thumb. I pointed down Broadway in the opposite direction of the train I knew he needed to take. "See you tomorrow, Cooper." With that I turned and walked away.

The day was cool but comfortable. The breeze was oceanic. The sky was blue and spotted with car, money, and sailboat shaped clouds. The trees—what few of them I could find—had started changing their leaves from green to orange, red, and brown. It was a beautiful day. I was glad that I had gotten caught up in a lie.

It had been a long time since I had gone *down* that street. I had quit my walks. I stopped exploring when I got hired at PaperClips. Walks no longer fit into my routine.

I went to work and I went home. I traveled the same route. Usually I even took the same train car. Sometimes I walked around Columbus Circle. On those days when I had a lot of coffee or the spirit moved me I might even dip into the Columbus Circle corner of Central Park. But, even when I did dip, it was never deeply.

I was wearing tattered shoes and my uniform as I walked. That was all I seemed to ever wear. On outings with Sofia or the occasional weekend trip to the grocery store, I'd slide on a pair of faded jeans and a plain threadbare t-shirt: clothes held over from my days in college and high school. Held over from a time when I gave a damn about how I looked. But, these outings were rare. I left the house as infrequently as possible. Fearful: I hid myself away from the world.

Normally, when I was outside, I was in my uniform. This is not to say I put it on to go out, simply that I only went out when I had it on. Usually I just sat at home bare-chested and in shorts.

I would take the train down to 59th and walk a block down Broadway to PaperClips. One block; no farther. I went to work for the scheduled time. Sometimes a little more if so required. Then, I simply reversed the process. I walked up Broadway, then I took the train uptown. I went down that road as far as I needed and then I turned around and went back the way I came. That was the way it had been for six months. It had been that way with little deviation until that day. Until I got caught in a lie with Cooper.

Down this road was Times Square. I could see the top of its buildings as I walked. It was close. If it was the country, and the distance from myself to them was composed of grass instead of glass and steel walls, I think I could have thrown a football to the square. At the very least I could have communicated over the distance. I could have yelled. On a country field, I could have thrown my voice at least that far, probably farther. But this was not a country field. It was a city street. In that environment, I could not even hail a taxi over the cacophony of voices, traffic, and construction.

Throwing a football? Completely out of the question. The ball would hit someone and I would get arrested for assault. To make things worse the ball would probably hit an executive. Then, in addition to being arrested, the suit would sue me.

No, I thought. *I'll keep my hands in my pockets and my mouth shut.*

I dodged and weaved around pedestrians. I tried to avoid eye and body contact, but failed.

"Watch it," grunted a man who stepped on my toe. I gazed after him in disbelief as he walked away and, not paying attention, nearly tipped over a baby carriage. I lunged with my hands, grabbed the carriage, and corrected its lean. As soon as I did a ravenous, bearded muzzle, reached for me. The teeth in its mouth were yellow and caked with black plaque at the base. I had but a moment to comprehend that the carriage's passenger was not a child but a Schnauzer. Its eyes were white with cataracts and most of its beard was gray. The dog barked hoarsely and began retching like it was trying to cough up a cat or—if the carriage was any indication—a rattle. The woman pushing the carriage had deeply wrinkled skin. She wore a bright red lipstick that matched the blush on her cheeks and the shade of her eye shadow.

She scowled at me with what looked like a combination of disgust and anger. As she scowled, the deep wrinkles around her mouth and eyes split. The exposed lines of skin were an unnatural white. The lines contrasted profoundly with the painted skin around them.

As the old woman pushing the carriage grimaced at

me, in that brief moment, I was reminded of an old-fashioned porcelain doll. A sad thing—old and cracked in the face. Unnatural color cracked to expose the white lifelessness beneath.

"I'm sorry," I said as she crossed my path and descended the curb into the crosswalk to my left. She lifted a thin hand and waved me off enthusiastically. Her hand was that same porcelain white.

"Did you see that? He almost killed that baby," someone said behind me. I did my best not to make eye contact with the voice's owner. Again, I failed.

I plucked the phone from my pocket. Its face was smooth and featureless. My thumb found and rested on the bottom center of the touch screen. If I were to look at the glowing surface I would have seen a silver button accompanied by pulsating white text that read, "Slide to unlock." I did not look. I did not have to.

There were two things I always had with me: my cell phone and my wallet. Over the years they had become a part of me. Natural extensions. I no more needed to look at my phone to make a call than I needed to look at my wallet to find the cash, or at my butt when I was trying to locate an itch. I just knew. Muscle memory knew. My fingers knew.

I slid my thumb—unlocked. Tapped the bottom-right of the screen—recent calls. Tapped again—"Ring-ring."

I was calling the first person on the list. The only person I ever called. All this I did without looking away from the sidewalk. All this I did while wading through a sea of people.

The phone rang once, and then went to voicemail. My call had been intentionally silenced.

I dropped the phone from my ear and it vibrated in my hand. The new text message read, "I'm working right now, sweetie. What's up?"

"I miss you, Sofia. Wanted to see if we could get lunch. I'm walking to your work right now. I'm almost in front." Before I could press send, my phone vibrated again.

A text from Sofia. It read, "I love you. I can't talk now. I'm about to go into a meeting. Work is busy today. I'm going to be home late. ☹."

I deleted my text and started over. "Okay baby. I love you. See you when you get home." Then, "send."

One block from PaperClips—and probably visible from PaperClips if the road were straight—was what claimed to be a pizzeria.

Pizzeria? I thought. *That's a stretch of the definition. Someone has some balls. Calling this place a pizzeria is like calling a gas station, which sells beer, a pub.*

The shop was small and decidedly generic. There were no stools, counters, or anything that could be perceived as an eating area. Behind the glass display case were two short men. One of the men was manning a microwave-sized pizza oven. The other took money with his left hand and dished-out pizza with the other. From his pizza dispensing hand hung a glove, which in addition to being much too large, looked heavy from the weight of thickly coated grease. It looked as though it would slide off his hand at any moment, but never did. He knew what he was doing.

Jesus, is that their only glove? How long have they been using that thing? You can't accumulate that much grease in one day. Can you? If so, should I be eating this pizza?

I decided to leave and turned to face the door. Behind me a jagged line filled the small store. I was trapped at the front of a hungry mob.

The one-gloved man asked, "Yessir? Whatwouldyoulike?" He spoke quickly and with a thick Mexican accent. It took me a moment to process and decode.

"Umm. Yeah. I saw on the sign . . ." I pointed to the door and continued, "Ninety-nine cent slices?"

He nodded three times and said, "Yes. Yes. How many?"

"Ninety-nine cents . . . that's for plain, right? How much for pepperoni?" I asked, while looking around for a menu or food list.

He was interested in taking my money, handing me a slice of pizza, and getting me out the door. It appeared to be a routine he knew well and was not keen to interrupt.

He nodded again. The nods were frantic. Impatiently, he asked, "How many?"

My reply was not immediate. I was still looking around for a menu. I found none. The walls were bare. The glass display case was bare. There were two men, a register, an oven, and five slices of cheese pizza under a dim heating lamp. Nothing else.

"Well, I want two slices, but how much is pepp . . ." Before I could finish, he had two slices in hand.

He slapped them onto two overlapping paper plates,

handed them to me, and said, "Two dollars."

His ungloved hand reached expectantly for money and lingered palm up in my direction. He pointed with his other hand to the person behind me in line. "Yesmam. Whatwouldyoulike?" I dropped two dollars next to the register and left.

Now . . . to find a place to sit.

Chapter 19

The pizza was every bit as tasty as moist cardboard. And, judging by how my stomach felt, it was just about as digestible.

When are you going to learn? Do not buy food priced at or around ninety-nine cents. It always ends badly, I thought as I rubbed my abused and tender gut. *When will you learn?*

I never did find a place to sit and eat my—disappointingly—pepperoniless pizza. Instead, I walked down to Times Square, then over to Rockefeller Center, and then back to Times Square. I passed photo shoots and movie shoots. I bumped into businessmen and got hustled by street vendors, which is to say I did nothing—just a normal walk around Manhattan.

Hopeful Christian

As I wandered, I began to feel bad for myself. Sad thoughts. Self-indulgent thoughts. I thought about my job, the uniform concealed under my hoodie, my halfhearted desire to be someone important, my daily—and all consuming—exhaustion, and, finally, my empty bank account.

Juxtaposed with the people on the street, I felt ironic, sad, and out of place. Everywhere I looked: happy people, smiling people, rich people, Downtown people.

I may live in Manhattan, but I sure as shit don't live Downtown. Others might not know the difference. But, New Yorkers? We know. We know the difference between Uptown and Downtown. We know the cost, and the value. Both financially and symbolically.

I live in Manhattan, but I live a million miles away from Downtown.

Depression and self-doubt grew in me until I could feel nothing else. I stopped being careful as I walked. No dodging. No more weaving. I bumped into passersby and gave those who dared to say something a hateful look, and, occasionally, the finger.

After exchanging words with a man who was at least as miserable as I, I decided to go home. *Fuck downtown. Who needs it?* I thought while choking back angry tears. *I do. I need downtown.*

Location was everything. *Was that not the reason I took the job at PaperClips? The money was a factor—of course. I needed a job. But, why did I choose that particular Paper-Clips? Why not one that was closer to my home?* I could feel my lips moving as I thought. People gawked, but I did not care. I was a man in crisis. Fuck them if they thought I was crazy.

There were plenty of PaperClips in the city; no shortage of demand for office supplies. I certainly could have gotten a job at one closer to my apartment. There were three in my area. Two just over the bridge in the Bronx, one on 190th street, just a single train stop away from were I lived. *Come to think of it, many if not all of them were hiring. I saw the Help Wanted signs.*

Why PaperClips? Safety. It was safe. Why this specific PaperClips? It was safe and it was Downtown. Downtown Manhattan. Finally, I could shout from the rooftops, "I made it. Be proud of me, world. Your son made it." *Only I didn't, did I?*

I worked in Downtown Manhattan. But, did I really *work* Downtown? *No,* I thought. *I don't work Downtown. I'm just* employed. *There's a difference. I am not unlike the guy who sold me pepperoniless pizza. We both peddle cardboard; his topped with tomato sauce, mine with toner. And, just about on the same block. No . . . I haven't made it. I haven't made anything.*

I was walking home; up Broadway. Fifty-second street, fifty-third, fifty-forth, fifty-fifth . . . beautiful. In-between fifty-fifth and fifty-sixth, was Random Home Publishing. The *Random Home Publishing. The Big Kahuna. The Big Dog. The big leagues . . . book publisher of my dreams.*

It was on the same road as PaperClips, and it was close. It would have been visible from PaperClips if not for the bend in Broadway.

A block from my work. A block from me, every single

day. Random Home Publishing . . . Jesus wept, I thought.

1745 Broadway, at the base of a skyscraper, huge sheets of glass kept my dream visible but beyond reach. I stopped walking. I stopped pushing downstream and started elbowing my way across foot traffic. *Must get to the glass,* I thought as people tripped over me.

"Yo, watch it," boomed a man in a gray wife beater and tight blue jeans. The man's hair was gelled up into threatening spikes. Spikes that looked like they would cut if touched and the resulting wound would instantly become infected. I ignored him and pushed on, until, finally, I was against it.

I pushed my face to the glass, like a child window-shopping into a candy store. My eyes drooled.

Behind the glass was a lobby as big as my entire PaperClips Copy and Print shop. In the center of the room, toward the back, was a long desk. A single man sat behind the desk. He was well dressed, well groomed, and handsome. The walls of the lobby were enormous bookshelves; wall to wall and floor to ceiling. Books and books and books. Hundreds, maybe thousands, possibly even a bazillion.

To the right and left of the desk were turnstiles. Only they were nicer than that. They were automated bouncers. Well-dressed men and women flashed identifications and the metal arms dropped, granting admittance into whatever magical world lie beyond. My eyes continued to drool. Salty rivers ran down my cheeks.

Did I know, when I applied, that I would be working practically next-door to this? Did I know that my dream job was only a block away? Did I want to be close to it because it was beautiful? Because it might inspire me? Give me hope? Or was it to punish myself? Rub it in my face. Keep it close. Keep the shame alive. *I'd forgotten it was here,* I thought. *I had avoided going down this way since I got hired.* This realization made me think it was the latter: Punishment.

It was a punishment I could not bear. So I avoided the building and blocked it from my mind. *Sometimes the heart knows when to stay away,* I thought. *Sometimes it knows its limits. Sometimes . . .*

I wiped the tears from my face.

"It's time to go home," I said softly.

I turned away from the building and reintegrated myself into the stream of pedestrians.

The cars had the light so I stopped at the corner and looked around. This was my block; where I worked. I recognized all of the landmarks, streets, and avenues. This was where I worked, but I was seeing it from a new and different angle.

Standing there, waiting for the light to change, I thought, *How funny . . . that a place can change so much just by viewing it from a different angle. Viewing it south to north instead of north to south.* How different indeed.

A lamppost—that I saw everyday—caught my eye. It was metal and thick. On the side I was looking at—the south side—was a sheet of paper. It was old and water-wrinkled. The ink had faded but had not dripped. *It had to have been printed on a laser printer. Not an inkjet.*

Inkjets lay down wet ink that, given the right conditions, wash away. Laser printers lay down something like colored sand. After receiving the sandy substance, the paper goes through what is called a Fuser. The Fuser is an oven that flash-cooks the sand to the paper. *Fuses* the sand to the paper.

This knowledge came from my experience at PaperClips. One of our Xerox printers was prone to jamming, and I often had to fish smoldering sheets from the jammed paper-oven.

The paper was taped to the poll at the top and cut vertically at the bottom. These cuts made little tabs. It was the kind of thing you might find in college dorms or shopping centers: "Babysitter for hire. Pull off number at bottom." Or "PlayStation for sale! Perfect working condition. Email Mike. Take address at the bottom." Only this flyer was old.

It was wrinkled and sun-bleached, yet not a single tab had been ripped off. I shuffled through the crowd and made my way over for a closer look. "Writers wanted. Come to open mic night and read your poetry or short stories. Thursdays at 7pm." It was currently Thursday and five o'clock.

I ripped off a tab. The tab was brittle and felt like a dried leaf in my hand, but the address printed on its surface was still legible. The event was located downtown. Deep downtown. South of Houston; SoHo is what the locals called it.

I have time. I could make it, I thought.

The feelings of shame and guilt were still fresh in my mind. I wanted to do something to make them go away.

Anything. Especially this. This was a gift.

How long had this sign been here? How many times had I looked at this pole and not seen it? What is it they say? Never look a gift horse in the mouth. My emotions were raw and I was not thinking rationally, but I was not about to second-guess my desire to go. I was in the mood and the mood now had an outlet.

I could go to work, print out one of the short stories from my keychain flash drive, and catch a train to SoHo. I could be there in just under an hour and a half. I could do it. I will. I'll do it, I thought as I approached PaperClips.

Tiffany was still there. She would be there until closing. According to Eric, this would be her last day on the night shift. Tonight she would work until close, and then come in tomorrow to open. I did not envy her. She would not leave until ten at night, and in the morning she would have to be here again at six-thirty. To compound the issue, she once told me she lived in Brooklyn, and that it took her two hours to get from home to work. *No, I don't envy her one bit.*

She was standing at the door greeting customers when I entered. It was her job as manager on duty. As the MOD, it was her responsibility to stand by the door and greet customers. *Them's the rules.* It was easy work. The perks of being a manager, I supposed.

"Hello, what can I help you find today?" After asking the question, her expression morphed, from fake friendliness to something a little more sincere. "Chris, what are you doing back here?"

I smiled at her and replied, "I missed the place." She

smiled back. "No," I continued. "I have to print something out." She nodded and greeted the next person to enter the store.

I went to the back, trying my hardest not to look at anyone. I did not want conversation. I could play the game when I was being paid to do it, but could not and would not do it off the clock.

Halim, one of the night workers, caught sight of me and shouted from the far corner of the production area. "Chris. Hello, man," Halim exclaimed in his strong African accent. I once asked him where he was from, but he would not tell me specifically—only: "Africa, man."

He pronounced man "Mon." Devoid of anything resembling an A, the word sounded pointed and subtly hostile.

"Man. I'm from Africa," was all he ever said about his origins. He never elaborated.

I only ever saw him eat Halal—street meat prepared as prescribed by religious law—and bitch about women. Aside from work, he seemed to do these two things exclusively. This made Cooper think he was from northern Africa. In his words, "A sandy region where women wear headscarves and men make all the rules."

In response, I told Cooper he was being racist. When he tried to defend himself against my accusation, I cut him off and said, "After all, I eat Halal food regularly. Lamb and yellow rice are delicious. And, Cooper? Don't forget . . . you bitch about *everyone*. Women included."

Regardless of where he came from, Halim *did* complain regularly about the promiscuity of American women.

"Sluts," he called them. His voice was always cold and certain. Halim's certainty that all American women were sluts made me uncomfortable, but mostly it made me angry. Not specifically because he was insulting *Americans*—but because he was insulting an entire gender.

He objectified women as a matter of course. No one was safe. I often wondered how he managed to avoid being fired for sexual harassment.

One day, while on break together, he told me, "Women in my country know to be conservative. They know that men are dogs and will take advantage. If men rape them? The women know it was their fault. They know they should have been more conservative. They know to be conservative and not go anywhere without an escort. They know that men are dogs. If they forget that?" He shrugged coldly. "They get what they deserve. Maybe sometimes . . . even *that* isn't enough."

This seemed like a foul view of humanity. And I questioned for a second whether or not he was joking. His look, casual and yet matter-of-fact, told me he was not. He had the demeanor of a man stating the obvious. Something everyone knows.

I remember thinking, *What about the men? Don't they deserve the blame? Shouldn't they control themselves? After all, they are human. Humans know better. Humans are not dogs. Humans know that raping is bad. Stealing someone's right to say no . . . that is bad.* Despite my thoughts, I said nothing.

I wondered if he had ever raped a woman, but did not ask. Not because I thought it might be rude—

something about him told me it would not be. In fact . . . he actually seemed to be waiting for me to ask the question. I never did. I did not ask because, deep down, I think I knew the answer.

"Hey," I shouted in response. Through a toothy smile, I said, "Just came to print something out."

He lifted a hand and nodded. His look was one of warm acceptance. "No need to explain. Let me get out of your way," was the sentiment. He ducked behind the oversized table to where we kept the ink for the wide format printer. I heard him ruffling around. He was looking for a specific color. Our organizational process for storing ink was nonexistent. There was a pile of cardboard boxes under the table and each box contained a pile of random cartridges.

It will take him a while, I thought.

The manuscript was fourteen pages long and took all of twenty seconds to print on the industrial, black-and-white Xerox. Adding the thirty seconds it took me to put thirty-two pound, cream, résumé paper into the bypass tray (only the best for my own prints; perks of the job), I was done in under a minute.

I shoved the unstapled sheets into a brown paper envelope and began walking to the register. Out of the corner of my eye I saw Halim. Now standing, he was looking triumphantly at a small white box. He tilted the box in his hand and I could see "Cyan" printed in bold blue letters.

Halim and I worked opposite shifts. We rarely saw each other, and, for this, I was grateful. We usually did not talk and I did not want to start now. I walked faster.

Tiffany was at the register when I got there. She looked at me with a smirk and asked, "Find everything you were looking for? Would you like to buy the pen of the month?" We both laughed at this. Real laughter. It felt good. Standing there I could not recall the last time I had laughed. I fake laughed often. It was part of my job. The smile was part of my uniform, after all. That was what the manual said. But the last time I really laughed? I could not remember. There and then . . . that might have been my first time.

Behind me, someone cleared his or her throat. I did not look but I suspected that a line had developed. "Fourteen sheets of black and white, on résumé paper," I told her as I extracted my wallet from my back pocket.

She looked at me and asked, "Are you serious?"

Unsure, I began to stammer, "I . . . I think . . . yeah . . . fourteen pages. I mean . . . I can recount . . . if you want."

Visibly offended, she said, "Come on. You for real? I'm not going to charge you for a couple of black and whites."

"Really?" I asked.

"You know how many photos I print for myself?" I did not. "A lot," she said earnestly.

"Thanks, Tiffany." I put my wallet back into my pocket, and then reached for the brown envelope I had placed on the counter. She beat me to it. She picked it up and then handed it to me.

Our fingers touched. They touched and pressed. Stroked . . . stroked and lingered. The touch only lasted a moment, but its meaning was unmistakable.

The look on her face was that of a person reading an engaging novel. Her eyes were wide and unblinking. She was reading my face. She was waiting to see what would happen next.

"I really should get going," I said. "I have to get down to SoHo before seven."

Disappointment. It was subtle, but I could see it on her face. It was just behind her smile. Just behind the uniform.

"Okay," She said. "Don't stay out too late. We open together in the morning. Don't forget."

I yelled over my shoulder as I walked away, "I'll be here."

I always am.

Chapter 20

The room was big—really big. It reminded me of a World War II factory. I imagined women, strong and sweaty, assembling tanks and artillery. The reality was much less dramatic.

"Welcome," greeted a thin, weasel of a man. His eyes, distorted through thick eyeglass lenses, were all brown; no white. He wore a short-sleeved dress shirt and jeans. His tie was thin and covered in a repeating printed pattern of old-fashioned typewriters.

"I think this is the right place. I found your flyer . . . I. Um. I. I. I came here to read." I spoke, but he did not seem to understand. Silent and with giant, unblinking eyes, he stared. "I have something to read. A short story." I continued to explain myself. Lips pressed tightly together, he continued to stare. "I have a short story. For . . . um . . . open mic. Open mic, right? People come here to read their stuff?" Still nothing. I turned to leave.

"Yes." He shook his head. "Of course. This is the right place. It's just . . . we so rarely get new people. Normally, it's just a few regulars."

"Well? Can I read here or not? Your flyer said . . ." He cut me off.

"No. Yes, of course. Please come in. Let me stamp your hand." I outstretched my hand and he picked up one of the two stamps that were sitting atop a wooden barstool. "Now don't wipe this off. Your stamp is pink. This means you are a speaker. They won't let you on stage without it." He stamped my hand with a pink butterfly. I blew on the wet ink as he put down the stamp and picked up a flash-card-sized spiral notebook.

He prepared to write and asked, "Your name is . . ."

Still blowing on my hand, I said, "Chris . . . Chris Christian." He looked at me skeptically. "That's my name," I insisted. His expression and nod said that though he did not believe me, he was still willing to play along.

"Now . . ." He paused, looked at the name that he had just written into the book, then continued, "Chris? What is the title of the piece you will be reading tonight?"

"It? It's called 'The Kiss.'" He let out a small giggle. "It's a short story," I explained. He nodded. He was writing the name and smiling. "It's a horror story." Still smiling, he licked his pencil and wrote in parenthesis, *Horror*. "People like it," I said defensively.

"Sure they do, kid."

"Honestly. It is good."

He smiled and wrinkled his nose. It was hard to understand his expression. But, I could not help but feel insulted. I wanted to punch him in his narrow face.

"I look forward to hearing it . . ." He looked back at his notepad, through his coke bottle lenses, and said, "Chris. I look forward to hearing it."

I began to walk into the room, but he quickly blocked my path. "One last thing. What is your email address?" He explained it was for the club's mailing list. I told him and he wrote it down on the sheet. "Don't worry," He assured me. "We don't email that often. Just a monthly event calendar." He ripped the sheet from the notebook and handed it to me. "Now head inside and give this to the man next to the stage."

The stage was a small carpeted area, atop of what appeared to be milk crates painted silver. To its left stood a hulk of a man. I approached him slowly.

"Excuse me," I said. "Are you the person I give this to?" He looked down and I felt small. "The . . . the man at the door . . . the guy with the glasses. He, um . . . gave me this. Said to give it to the guy by the stage. Is that you?" He nodded and pointed to the side of his head, to an earpiece with a pulsing blue light.

He spoke, but not to me. "Listen, I'm working. You only have the kids for a few hours." He extended a giant palm in my direction. The skin was dry, the grooves deep. I placed the paper into his hand. It looked like a snowflake against his dark brown skin.

"Listen. I take care of them. You didn't want anything to do with the kids after the divorce . . . no, listen . . . I have no problem with our agreement. I am more than happy with it. I love the kids. I am happy to keep them. Believe me, I am overjoyed. I love having them in the house. But you have to understand . . . I am working. Someone has to pay the bills." He paused, listened to the voice in his ear, and looked vaguely sad. "Listen. I didn't mean anything by that. I know you're going through some stuff right now." He paused again. "I'm sorry. Please, I'm working. I'll be home as soon as I can." Another pause. "You don't have to buy them food. There are fish sticks in the freezer. Kelly knows how to make them."

After another—longer—pause, he continued, "I know. And, I thank you. Please . . . just give them the fish sticks and put them to bed at nine. They have school in the morning." Another pause.

"Thank you. I'll see you when I get home. Call me if anything happens." Obviously impatient, he nodded and said, "Okay. Thanks again. See you when I get home." The blue light went away.

He looked down at me and said, "Yeah. I call out the names. A few people are in line before you, though. It should be about a half an hour or so. Listen for me to call your name. We serve beer in the back. Take a seat and relax." I thanked him and went to the bar.

I flagged down the heavily tattooed bartender and

asked, "Can I get a beer with a shot of whisky in it?"

"Sure. One boilermaker coming right up."

I turned to survey the room.

"Here you go," I heard a voice say behind me.

"Wow. You are quick."

"I've had a lot of practice," he said, setting my drink down on the counter.

"You want to pay now? Or, are you opening a tab?" I handed him my credit card.

"Let me open a tab . . . and, just to make things easier for you." I pointed to my drink. "I'm going to keep ordering the same thing." He nodded. "So. Keep them coming, wouldya?" He nodded again and I slapped a ten-dollar tip onto the counter. "Thanks," I said. "See you in a couple of minutes." It was not even a minute before I came back for a refill.

It took longer than estimated for my name to be called. When finally summoned to the stage, I was twelve boilermakers deep. In other words: drunk. Not black-out drunk. But, feeling good. Feeling really good. I was ready for the stage.

As I approached the stage, I could see that the big man was on his phone again. He sounded unhappy. "Listen. You have to put them to bed at nine. Jesus, Monica. They have school in the morning. You may not care about their education but I . . ." His words faded as I reached the microphone.

"Thud.   Thud.   Thud,   thud,   thud, thudthudthudthud." The sound of my heart pounded in my ears and made me deaf to the world.

Standing on the stage, I was only a foot higher than everyone else, but I was high enough to see that no one was paying attention to me. Anger gripped me and I tapped on the microphone.

The microphone picked up its own sound from the speakers. It produced sound, and thirstily drank the sound back up. The resulting whine grew slowly at first, then faster. The feedback loop hissed, loud and obnoxious. It reached a fever pitch and my heart stopped. Suddenly, I felt sober. In that moment I remembered where I was, and what I was doing.

Fuck.

I looked out onto the crowd. Not a happy face in the group. I had harshed their high. I had broken their groove. Derailed their pickup lines. Stopped the fun. No one likes feedback. And now, no one liked me.

Silence.

The crowd stared. They dared me to talk. And, more importantly—after what I had done to them—they dared me not to. I had interrupted and I had to pay for that interruption. I was a performer. And, now I *had* to perform. To do otherwise was to incite a riot.

"Hello," I began. "My name is Chris. I am a writer. This is a short story." I pulled the rolled-up story from my front pants pocket. I removed the pages and let the brown, paper envelope fall to the floor.

"It is a horror story. It is also a love story." People

shifted in their seats. Those few, who had not previously done so, now turned their faces toward my direction. I got the sense that no one wanted to miss the train wreck. No one wanted to miss seeing me fail.

I closed my eyes and breathed deep. The microphone smelled strongly of beer. This reassured me. I unrolled the manuscript and read the title, "The Kiss."

I cleared my throat and began to read in my best southern accent, "'Why you acttin' like this? Come on, quit backing away. What's wrong with you, Meghan?' Silent, Meghan lifted a finger. She pointed out across the hot, sun-soaked beach, to a body bobbing face down in the salty shallows."

I did not look at the crowd. If I did, I knew that I would choke. So, I continued. I kept my eyes down and I read. "'Jesus, I've come out of my skin! How in the world is that possible?' Meghan, shaking, began to swing her head from side to side. Tears and screaming."

Slowly, after a long, deep breath, I read the last line of the story, "Then, she breathed no more."

The story was over, and I was now weeping uncontrollably. "He was toxic," I said, as I wiped my eyes and tucked the papers back into my pocket. "He was toxic and their love blinded them. Now, it is too late." I turned from the microphone and started to leave the stage. Through sobs, I said, "He was toxic and now they are both dead."

I heard clapping. Or did I? I was drunk. I could not

be sure.

I kept my eyes down and sprint-walked toward the exit. The night went black. I do not remember how I got home.

Chapter 21

"Why are you wearing sunglasses?" asked Tiffany. "It's dark out." Her voice sounded shrill and uneven, like someone who was speaking for the first time, and had not yet mastered the subtlety of tone.

Later, when my head had cleared and I could think back on that morning, I suspected that this probably was not too far from the truth. Those were probably her first spoken words of the day. It was early, and there was not much conversation to be had on one's morning subway commute.

I was leaning against the door of the store, with my eyes closed, enjoying the uncharacteristically quiet city street. I was not asleep, but to say I was awake would not be right either. I was in the in-between place. The place people visit just before and after sleep. The place where people become stuck when in the throes of a raging hangover.

The suddenness of her question startled me. My head snapped to attention, and my eyes bulged. I saw floating white orbs everywhere and began to sweat. My head rocked and I could feel my brain floating loose between my ears.

The urge to puke came suddenly and I was surprised to find that the prospect—of voiding my guts—filled me with excitement. *Puke. Yeah, that will relieve the pressure. Yeah. Puke. Why didn't I think of it sooner? Drain the poison. Relieve the pressure,* I thought.

Tiffany reached into her purse, pulled out a small ring of keys, and asked, "Are you okay?"

I could not reply. I could not open my mouth. I could taste bile on the back of my tongue. It was bitter. It burned. I held my breath, and nodded slowly. The only thing keeping down the juices was the pressure of air behind my sealed lips. I could not risk a verbal response.

She fumbled with the keys and I stared at her hands with desperately eager eyes. Still not breathing, I felt faint. Time stopped.

Finally, she singled out a key. It was silver and thick. Unlike the other keys, this one did not have teeth. It was a long, rectangular bean with grooves and pits along the broadsides of its shaft. She slid the key into the lock.

I could feel my oxygen reserves depleting. I would have to exhale the resulting carbon dioxide soon and, when I did, I suspected a mess would follow.

She pushed the door open and signaled with her free hand that I could go first. I accepted her offer. Under normal circumstances, I would have refused. Under normal circumstances, I would have held the door and insisted that she go first. But I was not feeling normal.

No. No chivalry that morning. No pauses. No hesitation. Hesitation was not an option.

I wobble-walked to the bathroom, locked the door, positioned myself over the toilet, kicked open the lid, and released. The puke was thick and brown.

Tiffany was in the break room, eating what smelled like Chinese food, when I finished retching. I entered the room, covered my mouth, and tried not to exhale stench in her direction.

I thought that I saw her looking at me and I turned away. *No face to face. Not yet. I'm not ready.*

Above the microwave were shelves. The top shelf was high and dusty from nonuse. I pulled over a tan, folding aluminum chair and stood on it. Still facing away from Tiffany, I reached back for a small bottle of yellow mouthwash.

I had purchased the bottle not long after being hired at PaperClips. I had celebrated the arrival of my first paycheck—one hundred and seventy dollars—by spending twenty-five dollars of it on expensive beer. The next morning I had a twenty-five dollar hangover, and a yeasty mouth. If I had been thinking clearly at the time, I would have bought a portable toothbrush and travel-sized tube of toothpaste. But thinking clearly I was not. So? What did I do? I bought, one-hundred-and-eighty-proof, generic mouthwash instead.

The bottle was every bit as dusty as the shelf. I wiped away the dust and checked for discoloration or floaters, and when I found neither, unscrewed the cap and filled my mouth. I was astonished to find that age had not caused the mouthwash to weaken in potency.

Jesus, how could I have forgotten that burn?

I sealed the bottle, threw it back onto the shelf, and speed-wobble-walked to the bathroom. Not bothering to lock the door behind me, I puked for a second time. When the heaving subsided, I was surprised to find that my breath did not smell like vomit. It smelled like cleaning chemicals. The yellow stuff had done its job. Refreshed for the moment, I wiped my mouth and went out onto the floor.

I was not surprised to find dozens of unfinished jobs in the production area. On the oversized table, rolls of wide-format prints waited to be cut; others waited to be mounted on foam board. Elsewhere, stacks of paper forested the room.

Menus—tall piles of thinly sliced wood—waited to be laminated. Reams of business cards printed ten up, on heavy bond paper, sat next to the Spartan9000 card cutter—a machine that jammed consistently and never produced more than eight acceptable cards per ten-count sheet. Wedding invitations waited to be folded. Books waited to be glued. Books waited to be punched and spiral bound. Books waited to be packaged.

Everywhere, something waited.

And they would have to wait a little longer, because—on that day—I was going to take it slow. Low gear.

I was running on fumes and if I pushed the accelerator too hard I was likely to stall.

I went to the computer and signed into the desktop. As the computer booted, I reviewed the newest entry in the transitional log. The short message read, *Sorry about all the work. A lot of while-you-waits. No time to finish everything. I stayed as late as I could. Sorry. –Halim.*

I closed the log and opened the computer's browser. A message exploded onto the screen. *Twelve new emails*, in bold red text. Below the email notification—also in bright red—were two other messages. They read, *4 new web submissions* and *Mandatory worker survey.*

I closed the browser and thought, *Fuck this. You all are just going to have to get in line. I'll get to you when I get to you.*

Tiffany walked up to me and I turned away. My breath had smelled acceptable enough in the bathroom. But that was a few dozen burps ago, and the smell had since returned.

She chased my gaze and asked, "Is Cooper always this late?"

I turned my head further away. Then I lifted—and spoke into—my hand. "Yeah." The word sent hot stench bouncing off of my palm back into my face. "He usually shows up, though," I added.

"Chris. What's with you? Are you mad at me? If this is about yesterday . . ." She paused. I could tell she was trying to find the right word. Trying to avoid anything that might incriminate her. The store had microphones as well as cameras. For "legal reasons."

Eric told me during my initial interview, "Paper-Clips takes sexual harassment extremely seriously. The microphones are to safeguard our employees. Everything is documented—recorded."

If I had known then what I do now, I might have laughed at the irony of his words. But I did not know. I did not laugh. Instead, shamefully unaware, I looked solemnly into his eyes and agreed. "Yes, of course. I understand completely."

I turned to face Tiffany. Speaking through my hand, I said, "It is nothing like that. If you really want to know . . . I'm hungover."

"Really?" Obviously relieved, she continued, "I was wondering why you were wearing sunglasses."

Had she not reminded me, I might have gone the entire day without realizing that I still had my sunglasses on. My senses were running wild. I could not be sure of anything. The world seemed dark. Sure, a little. But, I was too worried about my numb hands and the white orbs floating around the room to give it a second thought.

I removed my shades and said, "Yeah. And . . ." The world was bright now and I had to squeeze my eyes closed against its brilliance. "And, I think I am still a little drunk."

She smiled, took the glasses from my hand and lifted them to my face. Then, in one gentle motion, she brushed my hair aside and placed the plastic arms of the sunglasses over my ears.

Her left hand brushed my earlobe as it fell. The touch—soft but intentional—made the nerves in my neck tighten. Then everything tingled. Especially my curled toes.

"Still drunk, huh?"

I nodded to her question and said, "Mostly just hungover." She stared at me then. She stared and I tried to keep my breaths shallow, a task that was becoming increasingly difficult. My body wanted to breathe. After her touch . . . my body wanted to pant.

The production area, piles of unfinished work and all, was still a large, open room. A room with huge sections of bare floor. We stood in such a section. The closest blockage was the computer desk and even that was five feet away. There was plenty of room to move.

She brushed into me as she passed. Her demeanor was casual. She brushed into me like someone with a destination shoving by an obstacle in a narrow hall. My muscles locked. I stood stiff. I tried not to respond to her breath on the side of my face, or the heat of her breasts on my bicep. I tried hard to stay calm, but my penis fluttered despite my objections.

"It's seven fifteen," she said over her shoulder as she walked away. "I'm going to open the doors."

Chapter 22

It might have been that I forgave him for being crazy. It could also have been that the severity of his actions
had diminished in my memory. Probably, it was because I
just did not give a shit. After all, I had done worse.

Nothing racist. I tried whenever possible to keep
race out of it. Partly because I knew that I had the weaker
position; purebred-poor-white-trash was a losing hand.
Mostly, though, I just respected people. At least . . . I
respected them enough not to judge them based on the
color of their skin.

Why should I have to resort to skin color? Why resort to color when there are so many perfectly reasonable
excuses to hate someone?

Fights? Causing a scene? Making a fool of myself? Making a fool of myself on the subway? I did these things with surprising regularity. Still do. I figured Cooper deserved a pass.

We were walking but I made an effort to make eye contact. "Listen, crazy," I began. "People are going to stare. People stare. That is just how it is." Cooper nodded. He looked as though he had been expecting this talk. "You just have to ignore them. Okay? Fuck 'em." He nodded and I continued my lecture. "I understand that you get pissed. I do too. I hate those rubbernecking, bug-eyed, nosy fuckers." I said the words sincerely; I meant them. He seemed to understand and nodded again with enthusiasm. "You have to pick your battles. If someone steps up to you . . . fight. Fuck it. I'll help you." I paused and considered my words. "But *do not* start shit with someone who is just trying to get to where they are going."

We made eye contact and I saw that he had understood. I sensed relief in him. It was as if he had been waiting for my forgiveness. As if my opinion mattered. I could not think of why it would. I suspected he just needed someone to forgive him. It did not seem like he could do it himself.

We talked about work on the ride home. He told me that he thought it was hell and I agreed. He was yelling but I still had difficulty hearing him over the various sounds of passengers and rubbing steel. "I never thought I would be working at PaperClips. I always imagined that I was better than that."

"It's loud. I can't hear you," I said.

He tugged on his right ear and yelled for me to

speak up. I pointed to my book. He shook his head and shrugged that he did not understand. I picked up the book and began to read. This he understood. We stopped speaking for the rest of the ride.

Cooper was a man transformed. Our conversation had obviously put him in good spirits.

He spoke quickly and his gait developed a gentle pop that made it seem like he was skipping. "How do you like working with Tiffany?" he asked. Still nauseous from the previous night, and experiencing vertigo from reading on the train, I tried but could not bring myself to respond to his question. Awkward silence abounded. "I love it," he volunteered. "Work was so much less stressful today." To this I did manage to nod in agreement. "Shit. It was almost enjoyable."

Not ever wanting to hear enjoyable associated with PaperClips, I forced myself to respond. "Yeah . . . I don't know about that. Let's not get ahead of ourselves,"

"Yeah. Maybe." He paused, then continued, "What about Tiffany, though. She's not the hottest girl, true. But . . . have you seen her tits?" He grabbed at invisible breasts and, after a moment of groping the air, wiped at his forehead in mock exhaustion. "Phew. The things I would do to her." He shook his head and looked at the ground.

"What would you do to her?" I asked.

He looked at me wearily. Like he was second-guessing if he should even be talking to someone who did not *get* what he meant. Seeing that I truly did not understand he clarified, "I'd fuck the shit out of her."

Of course, I thought and realized that I would have known his meaning immediately had I not been fighting my equilibrium to walk in a straight line.

"Obviously . . ." I paused to take a thin, shaky breath, then said, "Sorry about that shit on the train. I couldn't talk. I'm hungover. I've been sick all day. You understand?" He nodded that he did.

"Yeah. I understand. I've got the same sickness." He lifted an imaginary drink to his mouth and took a loud sip.

I stopped walking, pointed down Vermilyea Avenue to Dyckman Street, and said, "I have to go to Duane Reade. I need something to help me deal with this headache." I started walking away before he could answer.

"Yeah. I'll see you tomorrow," he yelled. I lifted my hand and waved over my shoulder. I felt like I was dying. I needed beer and Duane Reade sold six-packs of Cherry Wheat Ale for eleven dollars. I purchased six bottles of hair-from-the-dog-that-bit-me and went home.

I was at home and drunk before I realized that Cooper and I would not be seeing each other tomorrow. Tomorrow was Saturday. Saturday was our day off.

This realization came after *her* text, but well before I decided what to do about it.

No. I would not decide what to do about the text message until much later. And even then—as I sat in that dimly lit bar preparing to cheat on my girlfriend—I would still be deciding.

Chapter 23

Four Monkeys was a bar-restaurant on Broadway, two blocks south of PaperClips. It was new and trendy. By trendy, I mean expensive.

The bar menu sported Angus burgers, oysters, mussels, and lobsters. Nothing was below ten dollars. Disgusted with the prices, I tossed the menu onto our table, between two small white candles. The flames flickered from the resulting breeze.

I pointed to the menu that I had just thrown onto the table and asked, "Did you know that I printed that?"

Tiffany looked at the menu and I saw a mild surprise paint her face. She looked like someone who had just discovered something funny. She picked up the menu and examined it. Not the words and outrageous prices—like I had done—but the paper and subtle letter-shaped bumps on its surface. She traced the M in "Monkeys" with the soft face of her left hand thumb.

Without looking up she said, "No. I didn't know. Boy would come in and drop off his jobs at night—the owner I mean—and I would take them in." She paused and I thought about asking her why she was the one who took in the order. She was service, not production. Taking in orders was something she was capable of doing—we were all cross-trained—but, as a rule, we stayed within our departments.

She looked at me as if anticipating my question. I smiled, decided I did not care, and motioned for her to continue.

"Dude's a nice guy. His orders are big. They end up being a couple hundred dollars." She put the menu back between the candles, looked up into my eyes, then continued, "He always comes in late. Like, just before closing. So we never have a chance to start his job. We leave it for the morning crew. And honestly . . . fuck. I always thought it was Maria who did his jobs." More than a little insulted, I asked why she thought that. "Because she hoards all of the jobs. You ain't noticed? She won't let anyone else do shit. It's like she don't trust anyone—or something . . . I don't know."

Thirsty, I looked around the busy bar—not a server in sight. I rubbed my throat, trying to stimulate saliva production, and said, "She *is* slow . . . Sure. But hoarding? Why would anyone want to make more work for themselves?"

She shrugged and said, "I always figured it's because she's crazy." Her eyes grew wide and honest, like those of someone eager to share some secret inside knowledge. "She is, you know? Crazy, I mean. Crazy as a son-of-a-bitch. Girl be fucking loco. I don't know . . . I don't know what is up with her but . . . let me tell you right now . . . Bitch ain't right."

It was on my tongue to ask her to continue when a tall, barrel-chested, thick-waisted, ponytailed man with a long white beard and rimless glasses approached our table and addressed Tiffany by name. Tiffany jumped up into the arms of this stranger and they hugged for a long moment.

Though his face was buried in Tiffany's hair, I could still hear him say, "Tiffany, what a surprise. What are you doing here?" She looked lost in the moment. Lost in his arms. Confused by his question, she asked him what he meant. "You're here. It's Saturday. You usually come on weekdays." Still hugging her, he paused and seemed to savor the moment. "You normally only stop by after work. What's the occasion?"

Their gentle rocking halted suddenly and she slid from his arms. She pushed her hair from her face and began to speak disjointedly as she straightened her blouse. Their embrace had been vigorous and the thin fabric was now bunched under her armpits.

"I am here . . . with a friend." She pointed to me and I waved. "This is Chris from work. Chris, this is Tom. Tom's the owner of this bar . . ." She paused. "The guy I was telling you about."

Tom extended a hand and I grabbed it. He looked at me with a quiet confidence and asked, "Chris?"

I nodded. I felt like a man who was meeting his girlfriend's ex for the first time. I felt my chest tighten and my heart race with anger and the faintest dash of jealousy. I squeezed his hand. He did not seem to notice. "You work at PaperClips? How come I've never seen you? Where you been? Hiding?" Obviously happy with his superior wit, he laughed openly.

I stared at him blankly and after an awkward moment reached down and picked up the menu. "No," I said. "I work in the mornings. I'm the one who printed this." He looked at the menu and then back at me. His smile relaxed. "I always do your printing." I threw the menu back on the table and he followed it with his gaze as it slid to a stop. "You could say I am your personal printer." I smiled then. Now *he* was wearing the blank look. Another awkward moment.

Tom looked at his watch and said, "Listen. I have to go work the room. I'll send a waitress over. She'll take care of you." Tiffany stood and they hugged again. This time there was no rocking and her blouse stayed in its normal position. She kissed him on his white, hairy, and slightly moist cheek.

I tasted acid in the back of my throat. I had to look away.

"Nice meeting you, Chris. Keep up the good work."

"You too, Tom," I said, still looking away. And then he was gone.

I watched Tom periodically for the rest of the night.

How he laughed and joked his way through the room—he had everyone's ear. People seemed eager to give it. As eager as Tiffany had been.

The room, though large, was far from huge. I had to try hard not to bump into people—even when sitting. Still, Tom managed to avoid our table for the rest of the night.

"I can explain." She had the look of someone who had been caught, but more than that, she looked guilty. Guilty and ready to plead for forgiveness. I wondered how often she found herself in that position. How often she had to explain and beg forgiveness.

She began to speak, and I cut her off. "I don't care," I said bluntly. She looked surprised. Obviously this was not a reaction she was used to.

"We all have our shit," I explained. "Fuck knows, I'm no exception. Let's make a deal . . . Okay, Tiffany? You don't tell me, and I wont tell you. That way, we all have plausible deniability."

Her mouth opened and then closed. She opened it a second time, clearly intending to say something, but after a moment simply closed it again. She seemed unsure. Contemplative. This game was new and I could tell she was having trouble defining the rules.

It was when she opened her mouth for the third time that a waitress emerged from the crowd that surrounded our table and said, "Welcome to Four Monkeys, home of the five pound mussel bowl. What would you like to order?" She pointed aimlessly over her shoulder. "The boss sent me over." Her smile was fake and I could tell she resented being "sent" anywhere. "He told me to take care of you guys." She pointed to the menu on the table and said, "Your first four drinks are free."

Surprised and amazed, I looked at her with disbelief. This was the best possible news. Perhaps Tom was an okay guy. Perhaps I had misjudged him. I almost felt like seeking him out and giving him a hug and a kiss on the cheek.

Almost.

I smiled wide and asked for the most expensive bottle of beer on the menu. Without looking at the menu Tiffany ordered something called Delirium Tremens. I expected the waitress to ask her what the hell she was talking about, and to order something on the menu, but no such thing happened.

The waitress took no notes. Instead she simply dropped the hand holding the notepad to her side and with the other shoved a chewed, yellow, number two pencil into her tightly drawn hair. She bared her teeth to us and vanished into the crowd.

Tiffany looked across the table into my eyes and asked, "You don't care?"

I shook my head and said, "No. Why should I?"

She said nothing.

"No, I don't care. I'm not the jealous type. And, even if I were, it's not my place." This she seemed to understand. "Speaking of which . . . how's your boyfriend?"

"My what?" She looked disgusted.

"Your Boyfriend. Your Man. Your Boy. How is your Boo?"

"I told you, he's not my boyfriend."

I chuckled playfully and said, "I could have sworn that I heard you call him that at work."

"Yeah? Well that's not what he is. We *are* close . . . but it ain't like that."

"What's it like?"

She looked down at her hands, which were on the table rubbing each other, and said, "We're together. I guess . . . but, only until I find something better."

"Does he know that?" Her eyes dropped to one of the candles on the table. She lifted a hand and held it over the small yellow-red flame. I thought she would move it quickly after feeling the heat. But she lingered.

I was about to grab her hand and carry it to safety when she moved it herself. The room was thick with hormones, cologne and the sweet smell of spilled mixed drinks. The smell of her burning hand overpowered them all.

Head down, looking at her palm, she said, "He loves me." The look in her eyes was cold. If there was emotion there, it was something like regret.

"Yeah?" I asked,

"Yeah. Dude's stupid."

"You don't love him back?"

Rubbing black soot from her palm she spoke quietly. Her words were slow and soft. I struggled to listen. "He's my first guy. My first dick . . ." She grabbed the candle and spun it on the table between her thumb and forefinger. She stared at it. Eye contact seemed to be out of the question at the moment.

"We fuck all the time. It's hot." I nodded at this but she was still looking at the candle and I doubted that she even saw me. "He gets a kick out of the fact that he's my first." Her look was one of confusion. Like she honestly could not understand why he felt this way. "He acts like he popped my pussy or something."

"Your cherry? Didn't he?" I asked.

She smiled but continued to look down at the candle. "No. A big black strap-on did that . . . when I was fifteen. I still have it. We call it Zeus." She smiled again and I laughed.

Still laughing I said, "That's the best name for a dildo I have ever heard." She looked at me. Our eyes met and then she joined me in my laughter.

"Who is 'we'?" I asked after a moment. I knew the answer. She meant whoever used it on her. A laundry list of women, slowly but consistently populated from age fifteen to now.

Her look said, "Wouldn't you like to know." Mine said that I would. We laughed again.

Wanting to stay on the topic of sex, I asked, "So . . . it is hot? How so?"

"I don't know. He's my first dick. There's a lot you can do with it." She licked her lips and pointed through the table at my crotch. "Plus . . . I'm a freak."

I leaned across the table, turned an eager ear toward Tiffany, and asked, "Yeah? Tell me about it." The light in the bar was dim, most of it came from the candles scattered throughout, and the skin on her face was darker still. None of that mattered. I could still see her blush.

"*Cum* is a new thing for me." She said the word "cum" slowly; adding eight U's and, at the very minimum, at least three M's. "Cuuuuuuuummm." I felt motion in my pants but ignored it.

"Yeah?" I asked.

"He likes to cum on me."

"That's normal . . . I . . . um . . ." I tried to say something more but—deprived of blood—the brain in my head was useless. The gorged, single-minded beast in my pants, the one that was now calling the shots and leading me down this dark path, was not much for conversation.

She caressed her cheek with the back of her hand and said, "He likes to cum on my face. Right. On. My face." Using her index finger, she traced a line around her face. She started at her chin. Slowly, the finger went up to, and circled, her mouth. Her lips puckered and she kissed the tip of her finger. Then she sucked it down to the knuckle. The finger emerged wet with saliva. She moved the finger along her cheek and up the bridge of her nose. Finally, she brought the finger to her open left eye. Like someone adjusting a contact lens, she applied what remained of the saliva to her naked cornea and said, "I like it too . . . it turns me on. It's hot. Like hot, hot. Temperature hot. Sometimes it feels like it's burning my face."

I could not talk. I could not say anything. I simply stared in disbelief.

She continued, "I love it. I love the way it tastes. I'm pissed I waited so long to give it a try."

She appeared to understand that I was speechless. The realization seemed to excite her. My face was hot and I imagined that I was glowing red. My face: a beacon of light in the dimly lit bar.

Seemingly eager to up the ante, she began again, but with a giddy enthusiasm. "He likes it when I lick his ass. Do you think its gay for a dude to like having his asshole licked?" I tried to reply to the question but only managed to stammer and mumble something about the prostate being the male g-spot.

Thankfully, as if on cue, the waitress arrived with our drinks. The beer she placed on the table was in a tall thin glass. The liquid was cloudy and amber in color. I drank it all before she turned to leave.

I stopped her and said, "The rest of the free drinks? Make them this." I handed her the empty glass. "Can you bring them all at once?" She nodded and turned to leave. I tapped her on the shoulder and she turned again in my direction. "After I'm done with the free stuff, just start bringing me bottles of Budweiser." She turned again to leave.

"Bud Light," I yelled as she disappeared into the crowd. "Fuck . . ." I made to get up and follow her; then sat back down. "Damnit . . ." Tiffany was looking at me—surprised and amused at my outburst.

"Bud Light. I'm trying to stay healthy."

The drinks were strong and my stomach empty. Two beers had the effect of four . . . and I was seven beers deep. A strong buzz. An informal date with a coworker.

Unrelenting thoughts of the woman I loved and lived with
. . . things were heavy and I was losing my grip.

How much longer can I juggle all of this? I wondered.
*How long until the axe, bowling ball, and lit Molotov cocktail
come crashing down on top of me?*

I felt as though things were going to get hairy . . .
deadly serious. One slip of the hand and it would all be
over. One momentary lapse in focus and everything would
come down. Everything.

But . . . I could feel myself growing old. Time was
wasting. Could I afford not to juggle? Did I have the time?
Does anyone?

Was the opposite true? Was I too old to juggle? Was
my nerve as strong as it once was? Was my skill as strong?
Hand-eye coordination and muscle memory are important
things to a juggler, and I had not practiced for such a long
time.

More serious than the danger of losing a limb was
the possibility of losing the life that I had built for myself—
such as it was . . . did even that matter? Did I care? Especially with a penis as lonely as mine was.

All of the questions; none of the answers.

Tiffany handed me her phone and said, "I just got
this text. I don't know who it's from. It's fucked though."

The text read: YoU ThInK YoU HoTT ShiTT?
YoU aiNt As sLIck aS yOu THinK. PEoplEs oN To yoU.
DonT WorRy. You GonNa geT YoUrs. KarMas a
BITCH!!!

I was astonished. Not just by the savageness of the
message—though that was certainly part of it—but by the

way it was written. Someone had taken the time and effort to change the case of random letters, yet they completely disregarded grammar, spelling, and punctuation. I did not know what to make of it.

Tiffany took the phone from my hand. After reading the message several more times she said, "How some letters are uppercase . . . some big some small . . . you see that? They obviously know me. That's how I text. That's *my* Thing. Ever since high school."

"Obviously," I said. "They *do* have your phone number. Who do you think it is?" I asked the question through the bottom of my glass as I drank the last few drops of beer. The crowd split for a second and I was able to see our waitress behind the bar pouring me another.

Good girl, I thought. *Keep them coming.*

"I don't know. Probably nobody." Her phone chimed again and she looked at the screen. I saw something on her face as she read the message. Surprise? I was not sure. I did not care. The waitress came with a refill and I finished it in a small number of gulps.

Tiffany put the phone into her purse and zipped it shut. "Are you worried?" I asked finally.

"No. Why? Should I be?"

I circled the rim of my empty glass—hopelessly trying to make it ring—and said, "You tell me. Do you think someone might be upset to hear about this little date of ours?" She looked over my shoulder into the distance. She had a thinly reminiscent look in her eyes. I let her think as I waited for my refill.

After the waitress deposited a fresh glass at our table, Tiffany asked, "How about you? How about your girlfriend? Think she'd be pissed?"

The Budweiser was a beautiful golden color. The glass was cold in contrast to the crowded and humid bar. I wiped the dew from its surface and licked my finger. Then I drank the beer. For the first time that night, I sipped slowly. I was drunk now. I could feel it. The first few drinks had done their work and a few more waited in my stomach—in line to finish the job. I no longer needed to chug.

The beer tasted fruity; a subtle note on the back of the tongue. Something there and then gone. Something beautiful. It was the flavor of a new keg. A good batch fresh from the factory. Crisp and refreshing.

Had they all tasted this way? I wondered. I drank them so fast that I had not had time to notice. I assumed that they probably had been as good, and the idea that I had squandered them made me sad.

I tried to sound coherent. I tried to say something smooth. But, when I finally spoke, I stumbled like someone testifying a losing argument before a jury of his peers, "She . . . we . . . I mean . . . we don't have sex anymore. We haven't had sex in . . . forever."

I savored another sip, and then continued, "I love her. She is my best friend, but I need more than that."

She reached out for my hand and said, "Of course you do." I grabbed my glass, before our fingers could make contact, and took another drink. I finished the rest of the glass in three deep swills.

When I finally set down the glass, her hand was still stretched across the table. I looked at it—confused—as if it were the first hand that I had ever seen. She pushed it closer and I realized that we had not actually touched all night. Somehow . . . we had managed not to touch.

"She's never home," I explained. "I only see her when she's sleeping. She's like a ghost in my house." I looked for the waitress. "To make things worse . . . it's not in my nature to be monogamous. I have always cheated. Successfully too." I found the waitress and waved to her. She nodded back.

"Cheating," I continued. "It was like I needed it. I had so much of *me* to give. You know what I mean? Like one person wasn't enough." I looked into Tiffany's eyes.

"When I was in college," I began. "I had four girl-friends and two jobs . . . at the same time. And even that was barely enough. I have a lot of energy." Tiffany's expression said that she understood. "I'm hyperactive. Impulsive. Always have been. It makes me feel different. Pent-up."

I tapped my chest—hard—and said, "Here . . . I feel tight . . . here. Always. A fierce urgency. Like, I am ready to fight, or run, or explode. Something. Everything. I don't know what it is, but it's in my chest. I know that much. Just like I know that it won't stop. Ever. The only time it ever so much as relaxed? The only time I ever felt normal? During college . . ." I interrupted my own train of thought and said, "Where the hell is the waitress?"

After a long pause, I continued, "I had four different girls, each taking a full serving of Chris. All of them were satisfied. Some of them almost couldn't handle it. For them it was like touching a live wire. I could talk with one for hours about philosophy and existentialism. Immediately after, I would call another and talk to her about religion and science. Then another would come over and we would make love. And then I'd call a fourth and we would tell our secrets and cry together." I fidgeted in my chair. I was saying a lot. I was not used to talking about myself this much. "It was like they each satisfied a different part of my personality. I don't know . . . It was like each part of my personality was big enough to maintain a relationship of its own with these women. A whole life of its own . . ." The waitress came with my beer and I finished half of it at once.

"I think . . . I think this is what I need . . ." I pointed to both of us. Her and me. "This. I need this. Stimulation. Lots of it." I paused and watched the froth swirling around in my glass. "I thought that I could be monogamous. I met Sofia and I thought she was the one. The one who could be *the one*. I haven't cheated on her. It's been three years and I haven't. Not once."

I met her eyes and she smiled. A warm understanding smile. She whispered words so gently I could not hear. In the cacophony, I read her lips, "Until now."

I reached out and grabbed her hand. My thumb was wet from the glass and I rubbed the moisture into her palm.

"Until now," I echoed.

"Want to go fuck in the bathroom?" she asked.

I was on the verge of saying yes when her purse began to ring. I pulled my hand back and grabbed my drink.

"You should check that," I said as I picked up my glass. "It might be important." My penis felt fat. I pinched it and asked, "Which way to the bathroom? I'm going to go break the seal. I've been holding it in forever." Not looking away from her phone, she pointed back through the crowd.

When I arrived, there was a line outside of the door. Someone in front—a greasy haired white man in a beautifully tailored business suit—was bragging about his friend in the bathroom. He was yelling and I could hear his half of the conversation clearly. "He's getting a blowjob," he said. "No. She's a slut. I don't know. She works in our building. No. No, I don't know. All I know is that she is from the sixteenth floor." Just then the bathroom door exploded open.

A sweaty man in a blue business suit and a woman, with lipstick smeared across her face and neck, stumbled out of the bathroom. The man from the bathroom greeted his friends with a loud roar—a strange interpretation of a lion—and beat his hands against his chest like a posturing silverback. The girl with the smeared lipstick, struggling to retain her balance, took off her heels. The floor was wet from spilt beer and tracks of urine carried out from the bathroom. I figured she must be drunk to be willing to walk through such filth barefoot. The smell of her breath as she passed confirmed my suspicions.

I picked the phone from my pocket and checked it for missed messages. Nothing. I checked my email. Two new items in my inbox . . . spam.

I looked at the phone with disbelief. I was out at a bar. Cheating. No one cared? No one noticed? No one?

The line moved fast. Most, if not all, of the men just needed to piss. And when I entered the bathroom, I judged that most of them had missed.

The toilet seat was covered in droplets of urine. Some brown, others toxic yellow, and some clear. The floor was covered in what I imagined was a *warm* puddle. I contributed my fluid to the mess and kicked the toilet handle. The water pressure was low and after the flush the water remained yellow.

Careful not to splash, I slowly stepped toward the mirror. My face was flushed and greasy. I took a paper towel and wiped my forehead and eyes.

I looked at the man in the mirror for a moment and again pulled out my phone. Still looking at my reflection, I called the first name on the list.

I put the phone to my ear and continued to stare. The music coming through the door, though muted, was still extremely loud. It was difficult to hear the rings.

Through the noise I heard a robot say, "Voicemail" and then a *beep.*

Who is that man in the mirror? I wondered. *Do I know him?*

I tried to sound sober as I spoke, but it was no use. "Honey. I'm at a bar right now . . . I um. I'm with people from work. I . . . think I am going to . . ." I paused and broke eye contact with my reflection. "I think I am going to be leaving soon. Give me a call and let me know what time you're getting home." I took a slow, deep breath. Urine vapor filled my lungs and I suppressed a gag.

"I love you, baby . . . we should really try and hang out more often. I miss you. I can't help but feel like . . ." I closed my eyes and sighed. "I miss you, honey. We should try and reconnect. I love you. I really do. Honestly, you mean a lot to me. Okay. Talk to you later." I hung up the phone and left the bathroom.

I could see Tiffany talking on her phone. Listening and watching, taking everything in, I approached her slowly.

At first, her words were buried in the cacophony, but as I neared, I was able to single her out. Her words had an innocent, apologetic tone. "No. I'm at a bar with some people from work. No. No. It's nothing like that. Just friends. Fuck. Even my boss is here. Will you relax?" She spotted me. "Listen, I have to go. I'll talk to you later." A pause. I sat down.

She pointed to the phone with her free hand, rolled her eyes, then said, "Yeah, okay. I'll call you. Okay. Yes, I know. Yeah. Okay." Another pause. This one was shorter. "Yeah . . . you too." She hung up the phone and explained, "That's the boy. He likes to act like he controls me. Like he got a say in what I do."

"Does he know that he doesn't?" I asked.

"Who the fuck knows? Didn't we already talk about this?"

"I just had a similar talk," I said as I put my phone onto the table.

"Yeah? Was she mad? She suspicious and shit?"

"No. She's fine. Listen, I don't want to have sex in the bathroom. It's fucking nasty in there."

Impersonating someone trying to urinate while standing, she rocked her hips like a child playing with a hula-hoop, and said, "Yeah, I know. Dudes can't aim when they drunk." We both laughed at this.

I allowed myself to laugh. And the indulgence felt good. As drunk as I was, everything felt good. After several deep belly laughs I said, "Listen. I think I should just be getting home. I'm drunk."

"Me too. I'm drunk off my ass. That ain't no reason to call it a night."

"I don't know," I said. "I don't trust myself."

"So don't. Just let yourself go."

I shook my head and said, "No. That's crazy. I don't even have a condom."

"So?" she asked.

I looked into her eyes and said, "A minute ago I was going to say yes to you. I was going to bring you into the bathroom and we were going to fuck."

Tiffany licked her lips seductively, and then said, "That's good though, isn't it?"

"I don't think you understand. I don't have a condom. I was going to go in there with you without protection. That is how drunk I am."

"So?" she asked again.

"What do you mean . . . *so?*"

She looked at me like I was an idiot and said, "Just don't come in me. Pull out."

"You trust me to do that?" I asked.

"Yeah."

I lowered my voice, leaned in closer to her, and asked, "You'd take me at my word that I would pull out? Even though I am drunk off my ass. What if I didn't?"

"Then whatever. My Boo cums in me all the time. I haven't got pregnant yet."

My head snapped back in surprise and I asked, "What?"

"I think I'm sterile."

"What?"

She reached out, grabbed my hand, and said, "Fuck it. I want you to cum in me."

Suddenly, I felt trapped. The room was closing in around me. I had to leave. I had to get out of there. Things had become weird and I abruptly realized that I was twisted beyond belief. The room began to spin.

I pulled my hand from hers and said, "I have to go."

Obviously confused, and a little insulted, she asked, "What? Why?"

"I'm really sorry. It was fun. I had a great time. I love hanging out with you. We should totally do this again." I got up out of the chair. "Honestly, it was amazing. Nothing strange about me leaving. I'm not stiffing you. I'm not giving you the cold shoulder." Her confusion transformed to anger and suspicion.

I got up from my seat and said, "I have to feed my dog. That's why I'm leaving."

"You have a dog?"

No, I thought.

I pulled my arms through the sleeves of my jacket, and said, "Yeah. Didn't I tell you? Holden Caulfield. That's her name."

"Holden Caulfield is a *her*?"

I nodded and said, "Yeah. She's a bitch. Mostly she's a phony. I love her though." She looked confused. I pulled out my wallet and began looking for the fifty I kept stashed for spontaneous trips to the bar.

Matter-of-factly, she said, "I got it. My treat."

I put the wallet back in my pocket and asked, "Are you sure? I have money."

"No. Of course I'm sure. I invited you here. And did you forget? I'm your boss. I get paid a shit-ton more than you do."

Insulted, I asked, "How do you know that? I get paid a decent amount."

She pulled a credit card from her purse and said, "I've seen your paycheck . . . I'll pay."

I fell asleep on the train.

"Sit's las top." The words sounded distant.

"Sit's las top." She had a strong Latin accent, and I had difficulty understanding her meaning.

"What?" I asked.

I was still drunk. I had sobered up just enough to feel swollen and bad, but I was still drunk. I still could not think clearly.

"Sit's las top," she said again and pointed to our empty train car and its open doors. "Sit's last top."

"It's the last stop?" I asked.

She nodded gleefully.

"Thank you," I said sincerely.

When I sat up I realized that my book—*The Catcher in The Rye*—had fallen from my pocket onto the floor. "Don't want to leave you all alone on the train. Do we, boy?" I brushed dirt from its cover, smiled, and said. "That's a good dog."

I had missed my stop. Last stop was one stop past mine. I could have waited for the downtown train, but I decided to walk instead. It was only seven blocks to my house and I figured I could use the fresh air.

I got home to find that the apartment was empty. No girlfriend. No imaginary dog. Nothing.

I got naked, grabbed a beer, and hopped into a cold shower.

Chapter 24

It was seven in the morning when the chime woke me. An orchestra of bells ringing through a tiny internal speaker. I knew the sound well. I had a new email.

Not wanting to exit my warm, cotton cocoon, I lifted a heavy arm and fumbled through the pile of mess on our desk. The desk—small and cheap—doubled as a nightstand.

Eyeglasses, glasses of water, glasses of unfinished beer, bottles of unfinished beer, bottles of caffeine pills, travel packs of aspirin, dusty, unopened packs of condoms, a dirty sock . . . after a minute of probing I found the source of the disturbance.

My phone's screen was blindingly bright. I had

trouble focusing. Trouble reading. And, when I was finished, trouble breathing.

Mr. Christian,

*My name is Charles Lehnsherr and I represent
Modern Bookstore. We are a small publisher based out
of Manhattan. I was given your email address by John at
Writers Open Mic Night.*

*To be frank, I had the privilege of hearing you
read your short story entitled "The Kiss", and I loved it. It
is my opinion that you are exactly the kind of author we
are looking for here at Modern Bookstore.*

*This brings me to the point of this email. While I
would like to publish "The Kiss", we specialize in
publishing novels, not short stories.*

*This is why I am contacting you. I would like you
to submit any novel-length work, which you have
completed or may be working on, to our editors for
consideration (I will list the address at the bottom of this
email).*

*No promises, but if what you submit is even half
as good as "The Kiss", we should have no problem
taking you on as one of our published authors.*

Cordially,

Charles Lehnsherr

I sprang from my bed like a man waking from a nap
that had lasted too long.

I ran to the bathroom and splashed cold water on
my face. Then I went to the kitchen, drank half a carton of

orange juice, and scooped Chinese leftovers into my mouth.

Thirst and hunger satiated, I reread the message, "Dear Mr. Christian . . ."

Pure ecstasy.

I ran to our bed, shook the rhythmically heaving silhouette, and said, "Honey. Sofia. Baby?" I kept shaking and slowly a face emerged from beneath the sheets. The room was dim and my eyes thick with crust and sleep. I winced but that did not help my focus.

I thrust the phone out in her direction and said, "Look." She shrank away from the light and I apologized. "Sorry. It's bright I know." She moaned in agreement and closed her eyes. "But look. It's a publisher." I bounced on the bed, next to Sofia's head, and her bloodshot eyes sprang open.

"He saw me read my short story 'The Kiss.'" I held the phone in front of her face and said, "Look. He likes my stuff."

She moaned again.

"It's . . . look. He liked my reading. He likes my stuff. He's a publisher. He wants me to submit."

I sat down at the desk, opened the computer's word processor, and said, "He wants me to submit a novel." After a moment of searching I opened a document named BallsDeep.docx, and began to skim through the pages. "You know I've been working on one. I've told you that . . ." I paused, trying to remember a specific moment. "I know I did. I'm sure I did. I've been working on it for a few months now. Here and there. It's not finished, though."

I looked at the bottom of the screen, next to the

page count, and said, "I only have 34,603 words so far. I'm not even close to being finished but . . . he said in the email that I could submit works in progress." I looked at her again. Her eyes were closed and the blanket was drawn tight under her chin. Other than her head, she was completely covered by blankets and pillows. Even so, I could tell she was in the fetal position. Also known as the small spoon position. If I were in bed with her at that moment I would have been wrapped around her. She would be nestled against my chest.

We sometimes fought over who would get to be the small spoon; who would get to be small as the other person held them close. I usually lost. Even when I won, we always managed to switch in the night. Honestly? It never really bothered me. I was happy to be with her. Happy to have someone. Happy to be spooning, like only big and small spoons can.

I dragged the file over to my portable drive and, as it copied, got dressed. The room was dim, but I had no problem finding my clothes. I had gotten dressed, in both the dark and the dark of intoxication, enough to know the approximate location of all the essentials.

A box of text flashed on the computer screen, indicating that the transfer was complete, and I ripped the drive from its port and put it into my pocket.

"I'm going to go and print this out. I want to send it today. I know the post office is closed because it's Sunday, but I think UPS still delivers." I bent down and kissed her on her forehead. Her scent—musty yet sweet—filled my nostrils. I breathed deep and let the kiss linger. Her forehead pushed into my lips and she gently moaned.

"I love you," I said. "I'll be back soon. I'm going to go and print this out at UPS." I grabbed my phone and my keys. "I'm probably going to do a quick edit first." I kissed her again. "I'll be back in a few hours."

Unless it was cold or rainy—and sometimes even then—it was crowded in my neighborhood. Apparently, Dominicans liked being outside. They stood in clots on the sidewalk, sat in heckling huddles on building stoops, and played dominoes under sickly sidewalk trees. And, oh God, how I wished that I could have joined them.

I wished that I could have shared in the fun and the camaraderie. I wished that I could have been part of it; been part of the assemblage. I wished that I could belong. But I knew from experience that—despite being initially tolerated, and even accepted by some—my cultural differences would eventually alienate me from the group.

Despite being an outsider, I loved my neighborhood. Its vibe was different from that of downtown. People *moved* down there—sometimes too much. Busy people being busy. Sprinting. Sprinting to buy coffee. Sprinting to make copies. Sprinting, because they had long ago abandoned the idea of taking it slow.

People in my neighborhood had the opposite problem. They—at least those who hung around on the streets, sidewalks, and stoops—seemed to have nowhere to go, and nothing to do but talk, mingle, and party.

Downtown was loud because of traffic, construction, and the sheer number of people stomping down the sidewalk. It was loud because it had no choice but to be loud.

This was not the case uptown. We had fewer cars and fewer people, but those we did have produced five times as much noise.

In my neighborhood, it was always loud. An unending audio assault. Up there in Dominican-town, there was a harsh, discordant mix of angry noises, laughter, and raised voices; punctuated by the obligatory catcall. Children laughed, played games, and harassed stoic pit bulls and mangy street cats. Women drank homemade sangria and yelled, *"Capicúa!"* Men sang drinking songs, told unbelievable stories, and tried to get laid. And me? I walked fast and tried to avoid eye contact.

I made my way through the crowd and in the distance spotted an obstacle. Ahead of me, six men were wedged onto a four-man couch. The couch was black-leather and plush. It looked heavy and took up half of the sidewalk. The other half of the cracked cement walkway was filled with talking men. The men nearest the road were sitting on and leaning against parked cars.

One of these men was bending a steel radio antenna. The others looked, laughed, and cheered him on like drunken children. The antenna-bender's jeans were *designer.* They were covered in an excessive amount of buttons and zippers and, when he slowly slid off the car, I could hear the sound of metal scraping paint. I watched as huge gashes ripped their way across the hood.

Hopeful Christian

Most of the men were holding plastic cups of various colors, shapes, and sizes. Those who were not holding cups were drinking beer. A few men made the attempt to disguise their beers in small paper bags, but the majority did not.

I exited the sidewalk and passed between a car and a van. The van looked greasy. Black streaks ran out of every crack on its surface. A thick plume of fragrantly beefy smoke billowed from a revolving vent on its roof. As I rounded the nose of the van I could hear someone yell, *"Chimichurri con todo."* My limited command of the Spanish language told me that this meant he wanted something resembling a hamburger with all the fixings. The side of the van was bright with glowing neon words and, as I passed into the street, the words flashed into my eyes. For a terrifying instant I was blind.

A car honked and I heard someone yell, *"Coño. Yo te mataría!"* These words I did not know, but I assumed they translated to, "get out of the road."

I lunged back towards the lights that had blinded me and carefully felt my way along the parked cars. My vision was back in seconds, but the damage was done. People everywhere were looking at me with disgust. Mortified, I stared at the ground, as I awkwardly walk-ran away.

I spent nearly an hour editing the manuscript before I gave up. This was my first draft and—outside of the fevered act of composition—I had not read a word of it. If I had, I might not have been so excited about the prospect of getting it published.

My style of writing was haphazard at best. My process was: to write. Nothing more. I did not plan. I did not plot. I did nothing. I sat, and I wrote, and when I was done writing, I did something else.

I had tried plotting. I had tried editing as I went. I had tried it all and failed. What worked for me was: to write. The *only* thing that worked was: to write. A frenzy. A frantic upload of information. A race to document the thought before the thought evaporated. Before my brain went blank. I wrote to exhaustion or distraction. Usually distraction.

The end result of this approach was that manuscript. Stripped, hardboiled prose. Fragments. Excessive use of ellipses. Convoluted plot. Unending dialogue and strange descriptions. Not to mention the cardboard thin characters and their unimaginative names. But . . . coming from a guy named Christopher Christian . . . could anyone blame me? Regardless, it made me sick.

I fancied myself a writer? Why? *Because I wrote this? A child could have written this . . . no. A child would have written something better.*

When I finally printed and mailed it out, the manuscript was seven pages of edited copy—the first seven pages—and half a ream of fuming shit. I could not wait to get the awful thing in the mail, and out of smelling distance.

Immediately after handing my manuscript over to be mailed, I began to feel terrible. In my mind I screamed, *What have I done? Someone reached out to you. This was an honest-to-god opportunity to follow your dream and become a writer. To get out of PaperClips. To show the whole fucking world just how important you really are. And what did you do? Wasted it. Fucking wasted it. You piece of shit.*

The weather was beautiful and I decided to walk the long way home. It was not much longer—only a few blocks—but I felt I needed the time.

Walking this route brought me close to Fort Tryon Park; my favorite park in the city. The leaves on the trees had begun to change—reds and yellows. The tree line was on fire and I could not look away. So I decided to take an even longer route home. A jagged half circle that went in the wrong direction.

I could not help myself. I felt bad. Sick. Tight in the chest. I could not imagine going home. What would Sofia say? What would I say to *her?* How could I explain that I blew my one shot at success? Metaphor?

Would I tell her something like, "Well, honey . . . opportunity knocked at the door and I kept her waiting. She knocked for an hour, and when I finally let her in, all I could manage was to give her a steaming pile of manuscript." I did not have the strength to tell her that.

I did not have the strength to tell her that I was a loser. I did not have the strength to tell her that I was a hack. I could hardly admit it to myself.

This was time I needed. Time to walk and think—

reflect. Think about my mistakes and how I could regroup and rebuild. Contemplate where to go from here and how to get started.

Slowly—as I walked—I began to feel better. Air, fresh from the park and the Hudson River, reminded me of my childhood—of time alone in the woods. It reminded me of exploring. The adolescent hope that the world was just over the next fallen tree, just around the next pond, just waiting to be discovered. In that moment I felt hope.

"Maricon! You must be lost, Whiteboy." The words exploded in my periphery. I barely had time to dodge the projectile. The thrown object shattered against the stone park fence to my right. Brown liquid covered me. It got into my eyes and burned.

The car, containing the people who had yelled and thrown the bottle, sped away. As they left I heard laughter and Reggaeton music.

My eyes burned and I wiped at them with my shirt. The fluid was all over me and, as soon as I wiped my eyes, more dripped down from my scalp and forehead to fill the gap.

It was booze. It was alcohol. I knew that smell well. I searched with weeping eyes through the debris. The label was wet and clung to shards of broken glass, but the ink was solid; the words had not run. They read, "Brugal. Dominican Rum. Founded in 1888"

Still wiping my eyes, I thought, *Brugal. I love Brugal.*

It was then that I decided to go home. I had had my fill of being outdoors.

Outdoors? In the city there was no such thing. It was all just one big indoors. It was like college in that regard. Our apartments were our dorm rooms . . . and the streets and parks? Nothing more than a bunch of glorified halls and common areas. You could not get away.

Nowhere was pristine. Nothing was undiscovered. Nothing new. Someone had everyplace staked as his or hers. And usually they ran in packs.

Cliques met and enforced their turf. Anyone who did not belong was shunned. Accosted. Beaten. And, if you were a hopeless, talentless, wannabe writer, hack named Christian, you had bottles of Brugal hurled in your direction.

It did not matter if the accosted felt bad, or if they were just looking at the leaves—they got theirs. And that day? I got mine.

It was definitely time to go home.

When I got home Sofia was on the computer. I could see from the door that she was multitasking. Email, spreadsheets, and video chat all open and running. I went to the kitchen and grabbed a beer.

I opened the beer, took off my shirt, and dropped my pants in front of the bathroom. Despite all of my noise, Sofia's attention was still locked onto the computer screen. Finally, unwilling to wait for her attention, I cleared my throat and said, "I'm going to take a shower. I just got hatecrimed because I'm white." I heard the typing and video conversation cease. Then I heard the computer turn off.

"So . . . yeah . . . I'm covered in Brugal. I'll be in the shower."

Chapter 25

Work was shit. Nothing out of the ordinary, except for one thing: Cooper called in sick and Cynthia was covering his shift.

"You're what?" she asked, through a smile that was on the verge of becoming a laugh.

While printing emails and web submissions, I explained, "I'm English. My grandparents are fresh off the boat. I'm first generation American."

She began to laugh openly.

"What's so funny?" I asked.

"I tho't you was just white." Her English was broken but comprehensible.

"Yeah. I'm that but . . . I'm English too." She shook

her head and raised her arms as if to plead, "Stop. I can't take anymore." She was stupefied and endlessly amused; I was getting angry. "You do know that *White People* isn't actually a country, right?" She looked away and continued to laugh. I stopped printing and looked at her with both shock and disbelief.

Is she gaslighting me? I wondered. *Or does she really think that white people are independent, in and of themselves. In her mind did whites simply spring from nothingness? Could anyone be so ignorant? No. She must be fucking with me.*

I did not know if she was being sincere. In truth, I did not care. Despite her, I seized the opportunity to inform and educate. In my friendliest teachers voice, I said, "White people come from western Europe. I'm English. My tribe evolved in a cold climate." I pointed to my face and smiled. "That's why I am white. Less need for melanin."

She laughed again but harder. I felt my face fill with blood and my cheeks grow hot. I turned to the monitor and again began to work. I did not want her to see my face. She had gotten to me, and I did not want to give her the satisfaction of seeing me turn red.

Fuck her, I thought.

I stopped my work again and looked at her. I was serious now, and meant to have a serious conversation. I sensed that she saw this and watched as her guttural laugh thinned slightly.

"You honestly thought I was white . . . that's it? Just white. Nothing more?" I hoped that she would tell me that she was just kidding. Joking around at my expense. Trying to get a rise out of me. Mind-fucking me. She did no such thing. I waited but all she did was wipe a fat tear from her cheek.

I do not know why she was making me so upset. Normally I wouldn't care. I was used to being a novelty. I was used to being the token white guy. I had confronted worse without so much as a second thought. Why she was getting to me was a mystery. Whatever it was, I had rarely felt so defensive.

I stared with deadly seriousness and she seemed to try and calm her heaving. Apparently, it was difficult as she immediately began laughing uncontrollably.

"I'm English." I paused—choking back the anger. "More than that, I am an American. Just like you." I pointed to her. Slowly, her laughter began to taper off, and I continued, "Color doesn't matter. Race doesn't matter. Pink, brown, black . . . who gives a shit? We are all Americans. If you live here, in *America*, you are an American. And we should all be happy to live in such an amazing country. Where our national culture is: a mix of *every* culture."

Her eyes narrowed and she said, "I'm Dominican. From Santo Domingo." She seemed insulted. Pissed. "I was born in the Dominican Republic. I'm not an American." Sensing the weight of her conviction, I nodded. I perceived that I had struck a nerve, and I did not want to inflame the injury.

After a long moment, I dared to comment, "My girlfriend is Dominican." She stared at me. "First generation American . . . she . . . um. Her parents don't even know how to speak English. They came here to have and raise their kids. Now that all of their kids are grown . . .

independent . . . they are gone. They went back to D.R. to retire. They have an apartment on the beach . . . from what I hear . . . it is nice there."

Her stare chilled me. I had no choice but to keep talking. I did not know what else to do. "They worked hard . . . really hard. They worked in a sweatshop when they first came here; until her father managed to become a handyman in a building." Her eyes glistened like someone about to cry. I wished that she would stop staring, but she did not. "They worked hard. They gave birth to six children." I broke her gaze and began nervously playing with my nametag. "All their kids are doing well. They are good people." I was running out of things to say. "Like I said . . . my girlfriend is Dominican. Her name is Sofia. We live up in Inwood. We live in a Dominican neighborhood. So I am practically immersed in the culture."

"You think that gives you the right? To call me an American. To lump me in with those warpigs who kill innocent people for oil."

I interjected, "There are a lot of peaceful Americans. Not everybody wants to go to war . . . most of us don't."

She came closer and looked me in my eyes. "*I'm* Dominican," She spat. "I am proud of who I am and where I come from." She stopped and looked at my hand, which restlessly fiddled with my nametag. Her eyes lit, as if by fire.

Suddenly she batted at my fidgeting fingers. The force of her blow was negligible, but my nametag fell to the floor all the same.

I could feel the heat from her eyes on my skin. They were melting my face; threatening to burn my very soul. Without blinking, she continued, "Don't you ever assume to talk about me, or my people. Dominicans are proud of their culture. You think you know everything. You know nothing." She turned and walked away. As she disappeared into the break room I heard her angrily whisper, "Gringo."

I passed Tiffany at the register, and said, "Yo. I need to go smoke."

"You don't smoke," I hardly heard her say as I left the store.

I was shaking. My pulse—something hidden and usually never felt—rocked my body. My head dipped and lifted as it filled and drained with blood. I could hear the red liquid pump and swirl behind my ears. I was both anxious and faint.

"You work here?" I jumped away from the source of the question and crashed into a woman carrying McDonalds. She maintained her grip on the paper sack of food, but her drink fell to the ground and splashed my shoes and pants. The brown liquid—meeting little resistance from the thin fabric of my old running shoes—covered my toes and formed puddles at my heels.

The woman and I watched as the foaming fluid trailed its way across the sidewalk and into the street. I apologized to the stranger. Her reply was a smile. A gentle smile that seemed to say she was disappointed, but understood it was an accident.

"Let me pay for a new one," I said as I pulled out my wallet and handed her my only bill: a five. She took it and her smile warmed. "I'm really sorry," I said again.

When she left I began batting away the remaining droplets from my pants. The accident had arrested my attention.

"I asked if you work here." The man who asked the question looked familiar but I could not place his face.

I pointed to my blue shirt and said, "Yeah."

He pointed to where my nametag should have been, and said, "Oh. I wasn't sure because I don't see a nametag."

"Yeah. Sorry." I extended my hand in his direction. "My name is Chris." He looked at my hand and smiled. His teeth—straight and white—gleamed in the midday sun.

He looked at my hand and said, "Listen, kid. No disrespect . . ." He pointed to his suit. It was pressed and obviously clean. "I got a meeting. And I don't want to get soda all over me. Knowmean?" I dropped my hand and marveled at the perfect way his jacket hung from his narrow shoulders. My gaze dropped to the slight break of his pants and the shine of his black shoes. In my peripheral vision I could see my own tattered and recently moistened sneakers. Shame and shyness overtook me.

I pointed over my shoulder, and said, "If there is something you need you can go inside. We're not a full sized store, but we have a few things. We specialize in copy and print. If you need something printed just go to the desk in back and someone will help you."

. "Nah, kid. I'm good." He looked amused. "I just wanted to ask how it is to work here?"

I was surprised at his question. Customers asked me millions of questions a day, but never had anyone asked me that. After a brief moment of contemplating the question, I said, "It's all right."

"I mean. Listen," the stranger began. I've been in this store before. I seen the situation. Not a lot of men working up in there." His accent was thickly Brooklyn. "My question is . . . how is it?"

I shook my head, and said, "I don't . . ."

He pointed with his thumb through the stores glass façade, and said, "What's it like working with all them fine bitches."

"It's good. I guess. I mean . . . it's work."

He smiled, and said, "Especially that bitch who works behind the register. What's her name?" He snapped his fingers as he tried to think.

"You mean Tiffany?"

"That's her name," he said. "Shit yeah. That black chick. Bitch is hot. I'd give her a bit of the Italian stallion, if you know what I mean." I nodded that I understood. "Yeah . . . you know. You know what I'm talking about. A bite of my spicy Italian." I continued to nod. "My dick," he clarified.

"Yeah," I said. "I got you." I was more than a little uncomfortable at this point and was looking for a break in the dialogue to escape.

"You ever fuck any of them?" he asked.

"No." I said. "I . . ."

Before I could go on, he interrupted. "Well, you must have at least slipped one of them the finger. I mean . . . shit. You ain't queer, are you?"

"No," I said. "I'm not and I never did."

"With all them fine bitches, man? You never did

nothing? Not even Tiffany? Not even with *that* hot piece of ass?"

"No," I repeated.

"Come on. Nothing? Nothing with Tiffany? Have you seen Tiffany? Those perky, big, black tits . . . girl's obviously a slut."

I looked around, trying to break eye contact and exit the conversation, to no avail. Accepting that I was trapped, and that my only hope for escape was to play the conversation out to its natural conclusion, I said, "Honestly: nothing."

"Not even a kiss, bro?"

"Nope," I said. "Not even a kiss."

"You sure you ain't queer?" He chuckled, slapped me—hard—on the shoulder, and asked, "You the only dude who works here?"

"No," I said. "There are three others."

"You the only white dude?"

"No. My boss and another guy . . . he called in sick today, though."

He looked around thoughtfully, then asked, "That so?"

"Yeah."

He put his hands in his pockets and asked, "The other white guy . . . the one who is sick . . . he works the same shift as you? He works with Tiffany? Maybe he is fucking her."

"Yeah," I said. "He works mornings too, but I don't think he and Tiffany . . ." I was interrupted.

"What are you boys up to?"

He smiled with recognition toward the inquisitive voice at my back, and said, "Hey, Tiffany. We was just talking about you."

"Yeah? Only good things I hope." She leaned foreword and kissed him on the mouth. The kiss was light, dry, and short.

She began to withdraw and speak, but he grabbed her around the waist, and pulled her body tight against his. Their lips pressed anew.

As their mouths ground into each other, occasional gaps would form between them. Through these gaps I could see his tongue twisting into her. It seemed like hours before they finally separated.

"Chris," Tiffany said gasping for air. "This is Vinny."

Now I understood why he looked familiar. I had seen him before. Long ago, when I first started working at PaperClips, I would see them together as I left the store. Tiffany and I worked opposite shifts then. When I left she would be arriving. Sometimes he would walk her to work, and I would see them kissing next to the store.

I had not recognized him while we were talking, because that was not how I was used to seeing him. I was used to seeing his face wet and pressed against Tiffany's.

"Vinny," Tiffany began. "This is . . ."

Vinny cut her off. "Yeah, we met already." He paused and used a perfectly manicured finger to pop a bubble of saliva in the corner of his mouth. "Chris and I were talking about how sweet it is to be working with all you fine women." He smacked Tiffany on the ass. "You know . . . he ain't fucked with any of you girls?"

Tiffany, with a look of mock surprise, asked, "Really?"

He motioned in my direction, and said, "Yeah. Don't tell anybody, but I think my man over here is a bit of a creampuff." He looked at me and lifted a hand, palm-up, in my direction. "No offense."

"Whatever," I said and began to walk away.

He stopped me, and said, "No, that's good. It puts my mind at ease, to know someone like *you* works with my baby. Knowmean? One less person I gotta worry about trying to horn in . . . Knowmean?" Vinny leaned toward Tiffany. "Listen . . ." He sniffed and thumbed the side of his nose. "I gotta go." They kissed again—no tongue. "Chris, take care of my girl. Make sure no one horns in on my territory. You're a nice guy. I know you're good for it." He hit me on the shoulder again and walked away. We watched him as he left.

"You think he knows about our date?" I asked.

"I dunno," Tiffany said. "You talked to him . . . what do you think?"

I tapped the side of my head with my finger, and said, "I think he sounds retarded." She responded with silence. We both kept staring in the direction he had walked, though he had long ago moved beyond our sight. I continued, "No, I don't think he knows. If he suspects anything, it's not of me." Again she responded with silence. "He thinks I'm gay," I admitted. We looked at each other for a long, tension filled moment. Then came laughter.

Chapter 26

Minutes turned into an hour. An hour turned into a day. A day turned into a week.

A week of my life squandered.

A week closer to the grave.

I ripped the cap off of a fresh, forty-ounce bottle of beer, and thought, *I wonder what it would feel like to stick my dick into a tuna noodle casserole.*

Chapter 27

I could see the rain from behind the register; a rippling sheet of gray. A heavy, whipping thing. Fat drops exploded against street and sidewalk filth. Black torrents carried plastic and Styrofoam glaciers to thirsty drains. The city was being rinsed clean—washed—and I longed to join it.

"I love the rain." Cooper's words sounded distant, thoughtful. Still staring out at the rain, he continued, "Reminds me of when I was a kid. I used to run out of the house and into the woods. There was a creek out there. Normally the creek was shallow." He pointed to his leg. "Water only up to the knee in most places." He took a breath and I was surprised to see something resembling tenderness in his eyes. I watched him as he ignored the aisles of jockeying customers and gazed through the glass at the wet world beyond.

"But when it rained?" He shook his head gently, whistled, and then said, "When it rained, that creek became a river. I remember one time I ran out . . . I could hear my mother screaming after me. Telling me I was gunna get struck by lightning. That she was gunna whip me if I caught cold."

I watched his eyes as they danced in their sockets. Watched their frantic and futile attempts to chase raindrops. Still staring, he continued, "I didn't care. I broke for the tree line and was naked by the time I got there. A trail of clothes behind me; I was gone."

A customer came and I exchanged their money for a bag of goods and a receipt. "Have a good day," I said, through my regulation smile. "Try and keep dry."

The customer walked away and Cooper, in that same distant voice, said, "It had just begun raining. So by the time I got there, the creek was still shallow. Moving a little faster than usual, but still no deeper than my knees." Another customer came to the register. Cooper handled the transaction without speaking a word.

When his customer turned her back to the register, Cooper continued, "Still . . . it should have been deeper. The way that creek was . . . it was like all the runoff from the entire state got funneled down into it. Shit. I once saw it swell a foot from a five minute sunshower." He smiled. "I should have known then that something was wrong. But, my fool self wasn't thinking. I splashed around naked like it was the most natural thing in the world. And, in a way, I suppose it was."

A voice interrupted, "Do you have printers?"

I shook my head from side to side. "No sir," I said. "For that you'll have to go to a full sized PaperClips." I pointed past the customer to the door. "There is one on the corner of Fifty-seventh and Sixth. Only two blocks away." The customer, visibly disappointed, let out a heavy sigh. "It's only two blocks away, sir," I repeated. "You can almost see it from here." The man's shoulders drooped and he sulked out of the store.

Cooper cupped his right hand, scooped at the air, and said, "I got down and tried to dig a hole. Tried to make a pool. I was doing good, too. When *it* finally broke . . . I was in a hole up to my waist."

To my surprise the store had emptied. The rain had—in addition to cleaning the streets—cleared our store of customers.

Content to listen, I stood quietly as Cooper continued to tell his story. "Apparently, there was a blockage somewhere upstream, and all that rain had been piling up behind it. When that blockage broke . . . tell you what. Suddenly, I was riding a wave of sticks and mud . . ." A brilliant flash turned the world blue. For a breathless moment I stared out onto the street. Stared as backlit rain shone like diamonds falling from heaven. The boom of the thunder was loud and thick. I felt it in my chest. Somewhere in the back of the store Tiffany screamed.

"I remember laughing," Cooper said after a brief pause. "I should have been scared but I wasn't. There I was—buttnaked and riding a fucking tidal wave—laughing." He strained his back and smiled proudly. "I never went under. Not once. I floated on my back like I was floating on a cloud. Laughing the whole way. It was beautiful." Another blast of light filled the store. And another deep boom filled my chest.

Cooper's posture dropped back to its default position. Then, after several slow deep breaths, Cooper said, "At some point it dawned on me, that however far I went I would have to walk back. So I dismounted, and dug my way to the shore. Crazy as it may seem, it actually began to rain harder. I laid there on the bank for what seemed like forever. I let the shower wash me clean. It felt amazing. It was the best massage I ever had. My whole damned body tingled. That was when I got my first *real* hard-on. Or, at least the first one that I can remember." Another boom rocked my body. "I wasn't horny," Cooper explained. "But excited. Filled with life."

A soggy customer opened the door and disappeared into the self-service section. The scent of rain wafted across the room and I greedily sniffed the air.

Cooper, looking out at the rain, continued, "For the first time in my life I understood what it meant to be me." I looked at him but he did not return my gaze. "I found myself that day. Alone, naked, and dirty."

The wet customer at self-serve sounded impatient. In one pauseless burst, he yelled, "The machine is telling me there's a paper jam."

Unblinking and unmoving, Cooper continued staring out of the windows and at the rain. I waited for any indication that he was going to go and help the impatient customer. None came. Cooper remained completely still. It quickly became apparent that clearing the jam would be my responsibility. *Fuck.*

With more than a trace of sarcasm, I said, "Don't worry, Cooper . . . I'll get it. You stay here. Keep up the hard work." He did not hear me, or he did not care. It did not matter which. He kept staring and I went to help the soggy patron.

"Shit. Is it still raining?" Tiffany rubbed her eyes as she asked the question. It had been a slow day, at the copy and print center, and we were all tired.

I replied, "Yeah. It's crazy how much it's raining today. Heavy rain at that. Normally it comes down hard for a few minutes and then tapers off. Not today, though . . ."

She rose from her chair and, through a yawn, said, "I heard someone say it's supposed to be like this until tomorrow."

She bumped into me as she passed from the break room into the production area. She had her cell phone in her hand and the screen was lit and covered with text.

I followed her for a second before pointing to the phone. "Texting on the job? Watch out. You might get fired," I said sarcastically through a playful snicker. "Is that your Boo?"

She nodded.

I continued, jokingly: "Trouble in paradise?"

"Paradise?" she laughed. "Whatthefuck are you talking about?"

"Your Boo . . . things good?" I asked.

"Nigga's acting weird. I don't know what the fuck his deal is . . . talking about how I don't treat him right. Trying to make me feel bad for not saying I love him and shit." She put her phone into her pocket.

Genuinely curious, I asked, "Do you? Love him, I mean."

"What do you think?" she asked. With a shrug, I indicated that I did not know. "Shit. If I loved that nigga . . . I wouldn't be calling him my Boo. I'd be calling him my man. He *ain't* my man."

I raised my hands in mock defense, and said, "Chill. Relax. We're all friends here."

Her pocket vibrated loudly. She slapped the bulge—silence. "Dude's pissing me off. He's acting like we in love. Like we married and shit." Her nails were thick, long and bright orange. When she used the nail on her index finger to scratch at the tear duct of her right eye, I cringed in terror and prepared to catch the gouged out orb.

"Well, you guys *are* kinda dating," I said. "I mean . . . I know you don't think so, but it's obvious that he does."

She shook her head—hard—and as her large, golden-hoop earrings slapped against her cheeks, she said, "I don't know why. Tell him all the fucking time that we just fucking."

"He likes you." I looked into her eyes. "I don't blame him."

She broke my gaze and the dark skin of her cheeks

grew even darker. "I like him too," she said reluctantly. "But this is all happening so goddamn fast."

Unprepared for her openness, I struggled to find an appropriate response. "What do you . . . I mean . . . I don't understand. You guys have been . . . fucking . . . for a *while* now, right?"

"Yeah, but still . . ." With a look that was both shy and innocent, she tilted her head, smirked, and batted her eyelashes at me. "I'm . . . you know . . ." She sounded like someone who was trying desperately to avoid stating the obvious.

"Honestly." I pointed to my head, and said, "Clueless."

"I'm a lesbian," she said. I looked at her skeptically. "My whole life . . . that's who I was. A lesbian. My first kiss was a girl. My first fuck . . ." I now realized that I *did* know what she meant, and regretted that I forced her to spell it out. "It took so much work to *be* that. I always accepted myself. But the world never did. Still doesn't. I got used to it, though. Got used to being treated a certain way. Knowmean?"

I said that I did, even though I did not. Not really.

I had never been gay, and thought it was probably not something that could be easily understood by anyone on the outside. I figured it was like war in that regard. It was something you *had to do*, and had to do to understand. You went in, took your licks, rose to meet the challenge, or got killed. Sometimes, even if you did manage to rise— strong, proud, and noble—to meet the challenge, there was still the possibility of some asshole coming along in the eleventh hour to shoot you in the back. A raw deal, for sure.

Situations like that have a way of making a person stronger, at the cost of alienation. Acute self-awareness is an inevitable result. They had looked their enemies in the face and laughed—gotten away safe. These soldiers of dignity knew things about which the rest of us could only speculate. And I was having a conversation with a veteran.

"I'm a dyke," she declared matter-of-factly. "That's who I am. Fucking proud of it too—finally."

"You weren't always?" I asked. "But, I thought you said . . ."

"I accepted me," she interrupted. "Don't mean I was proud of me."

"Oh, gotcha," I said the words playfully and immediately regretted doing so.

She shot me a glance. Her eyes, cold and still, seemed to say, "You better be taking me seriously, boy." I straightened my smirk and asked her to continue.

"Took me a long time to be proud of myself. To *own* it. I 'came out' to my mom when I was thirteen. I came out young, but I wasn't comfortable enough to be with girls in public until I was almost seventeen. I was scared people would judge me. I cared about what they thought."

"What changed?" I asked.

She shrugged, and said, "One day I just stopped caring. One day, on the subway, my girlfriend wanted to hold my hand. And instead of pushing her off, I let her do it. People stared, but I didn't care." Her phone buzzed again in her pocket and again she silenced it with a slap. "That's what I mean about things going too fast. Fucking took me from thirteen to fucking seventeen to hold a fucking girl's hand on the damn subway. I need time to transition. Fuck. I might be a sex freak, but when it comes to relationships I take it slow."

"Sure," I said. "But I've seen you guys making out and shit in public. Obviously, you're transitioning just fine."

She rolled her eyes, and said, "That's just sex. Sex ain't no big deal. I'd fuck anyone, anywhere, anytime. So long as they hot. Fucking's no big deal . . . tell this nigga I love him? Call this nigga my boyfriend? *That's* a big deal. That's moving too fast."

I nodded, and said, "I can understand that. 'Love' and 'Boyfriend' are personal words. You're not there yet."

"Right. Plus, I'm not even sure if I *do* love him. He's my first dude. My first . . ." She reached down to her crotch and tugged at an imaginary penis. "How am I supposed to know if what I feel is for him, and not just his dick? I don't. That's my point." Her phone buzzed again, and again. On the third buzz she silenced it. "Plus, I am new to dudes. I don't want to marry the first one who puts it in me. I want to explore. Try different shapes and sizes."

"Catch up for lost time," I suggested.

She smiled warmly, and began, "I even thought . . ." She stepped closer to me and gently brushed the side of my arm with her fingertips. Her long nails scratched their way down to the back of my hand, and she continued, "I even thought I'd see what it's like to get with a white boy."

Her phone buzzed again, and this time she took it from her pocket. The screen glowed brightly in her hand,

and I watched her eyes dart from side to side as she read the messages.

"Motherfucker," she exclaimed as she ran to the bathroom. The door locked and, within seconds, I could hear her side of a loud, heated conversation. I decided to go to the front and give her privacy.

The front was still as empty as it had been earlier in the day. This was strange, as it was time for the usual midday rush.

Cooper acknowledged my presence, and asked, "Do you suppose something happened? Like, that something exploded somewhere, or a war broke out so everyone is at home watching the news?"

"I don't know," I said. "It's weirdly slow today, though." I tapped my way through a menu on the register's digital screen. "We have only made three thousand dollars today."

Cooper came over and looked down at the total. "Motherfucker. They're gunna have to close this place down," he joked.

I leaned on my elbows and looked out at the rain. It was still coming down hard.

Cooper rounded the register to stand in my line of sight. He snapped his fingers in front of my face, and asked, "After work, wanna go to the bar? Four Monkeys?"

"Probably not," I said, trying to look around him.

"Why the hell not?"

"It's raining a lot. I didn't bring an umbrella or any-thing. Plus, I only have my uniform. I don't want to go to the bar dressed like this," I said, and tugged at my nametag.

"Listen here, you little queer. It's just rain," he said. "You ain't going to melt. You never do anything. You're the most boring person I know . . ." He seemed legitimately angry at my noncompliance. "It's raining? I don't have anything to wear? Jesus, man, them ain't excuses." He pushed my shoulder, not hard, but hard enough for me to feel it, and said, "For fuck's sakes, you lazy sonofabitch, come out with us. Are you really going to pass up an opportunity to drink and unwind? Just because you're afraid of getting wet, and you don't have the right goddamn clothes? Christ alive. I knew you was a fag."

"Us? Us who?" I asked.

"Yeah. Tiffany and I were talking about going while you was on break. She was actually the one who suggested Four Monkeys. Apparently the owner and her are friends. He gives her, and the people she's with, free drinks." He saw that I was becoming interested, and continued. "That's right, free drinks. And if you come along? Shit . . . I'll even buy you a round once the free drinks run out."

"Make it two," I said.

"Done," he agreed.

Suddenly excited, I chuckled and said, "Well, I've never been one to turn down free drinks."

It was only a block from PaperClips to Four Monkeys, but the rain was so heavy that distance ceased to matter. One block, or twenty; we would have gotten just as wet.

The three of us huddled—soaked and shivering—in the doorway in front of the bar. "What the fuck is we waiting for again?" Tiffany asked.

"This girl I know," replied Cooper, who was looking around through the rain.

"Why can't we just meet her inside?" I asked.

Still searching, Cooper said, "She's beautiful, but she ain't the sharpest tool in the box, if you know what I mean. Girl could walk right past this place and never see it. Got to be out here to flag her down or else she'll get lost."

I was about to tell him he could wait for her alone, and that I would meet him inside, when he began yelling, "Michelle. Michelle." He waved his arms above his head like a posturing silverback gorilla—graceless and overly dramatic. Through the dense wetness, I could see a slender blonde woman wave back. She crossed the street and as she did I could not help but stare.

Michelle was beautiful. Her hair was naturally blonde, the kind that comes with matching eyebrows and a freckled nose. Her shirt—thin, white cotton with lace trimming—was completely soaked. The waterlogged fabric clung to her body so tightly that I could see the dimple of her bellybutton and the sharp peaks of her upwardly pointed nipples.

"Cooper. Tell me she's single," said Tiffany, who, I suddenly realized, was staring even harder at Michelle than I was.

Cooper looked at Tiffany, and I saw something there, in his eyes. A familiar look. A look that I had not seen since that awkward day on the subway. A look that I had not seen since he nearly assaulted a man for simply looking in his direction. It was an unthinking, wild look. The look of someone who was dangerous.

His lips thinned and quivered. "She's spoken for," he said in a low, serious tone. Tiffany, I think sensing in his voice what I had seen in his eyes, looked at him with surprise. Cooper jabbed, "Besides. I don't think she's a queer."

Tiffany, visibly insulted, turned and entered the bar. "What the fuck is wrong with you, man?" I asked.

Michelle was standing in the middle of the street, waiting for a break in traffic. She smiled and waved at us. I waved back and Cooper shot me that same wild look.

"Listen, man," I began. "I'll be inside. Try not to be a dick tonight." Not waiting for a response, and no longer interested in meeting Michelle, I turned and followed after Tiffany.

It was even emptier in Four Monkeys than it had been in PaperClips. I was not sure if this was because of the rain, or the fact that it was still only three in the afternoon. Either way, I did not care. I liked empty bars—still do.

Behind the thick, antique-oak counter were two bartenders, a woman and a man—both of them tall, thin, and attractive. The man pointed a cleft chin, covered in a fashionable amount of scruff, in my direction. "I'll order in a second," I said as I scanned the room. The man nodded and continued flipping through stations on a large television, which was hanging from the ceiling.

I found Tiffany sitting at the same table we had occupied during our *date*. She was even sitting in the same chair.

She spotted me as I approached, and pointed to the seat across from her. I rounded the table, sat down, and said, "It's a lot different in here when it's empty. I can hardly recognize the place without my shoes sticking to the floor, and people pushing me around." I rotated one of the two empty glasses on the table, and continued, "No candle-light."

The glass, though empty, had all the signs of once holding a candle: dried splashes of wax, soot from a smoky flame, and that familiar scent of burning.

She gently batted the glass from my hand. It slid across the table, hit the beer-stained menu, and slowed to a stop. "They don't put them out until later," she said impatiently.

"Yo," I began. "Cooper is a dick. Don't let him get to you." She looked past me and I turned to follow her gaze. Cooper and Michelle were standing on the sidewalk, out from under the protective cover of the bar's entrance. She had her legs wrapped around his waist, and was hugging his head. He was holding her up by her buttocks, and though I could not see their faces from my angle, I was sure they were kissing. If the motion of their heads was any indication, they were kissing enthusiastically.

I turned back to Tiffany, and said, "He's from the south. People from down there . . . they have funny views about the world."

"And can't hold their fucking tongues," she added.

Amused by her brazenness, I smiled, and said, "Bunch of maniacs—never learned how to be social . . . too much free time, and too many people shouting from soapboxes. I'm telling you . . . best to leave them alone and let them rage."

She shrugged meekly and picked up the menu. "I guess," she said. "And if he really pisses me off I could always fire him." At this we laughed.

"What's the big joke?" asked Cooper, as he approached our table. Still laughing, Tiffany and I shook our heads. He tugged on the hand of the young woman behind him, and brought her to his side. "Whatever, you fruitloops." He pointed to me and said, "Michelle, I want you to meet Chris and Tiffany."

"Hello," she said, looking back and forth, between the two of us. Her face was flushed, and since she did not seem embarrassed to be meeting someone new, I figured that her rosy cheeks were the result of her exertion on the sidewalk.

"Hey," I said, and offered her a seat next to me. She looked at Cooper—who nodded in approval—and then sat down in the tall wooden chair. There was a loud *thwap* as her wet clothes slapped against her seat and she giggled. Her laugh was small and innocent. Cooper rounded the table and sat next to Tiffany, across from Michelle.

Situating himself in his chair, Cooper grabbed the menu from the table and began to read it. "Michelle," he said, while browsing the beer section. "While I figure out what I'm going to order, why don't you tell my friends a little bit about yourself?"

She seemed excited. It was as if she had been waiting for this opportunity. "Nice to meet ya'll," she began.

"Like he said, my name's Michelle. I'm from Georgia."

"Just like Cooper," I added.

Her face lit up, and I wondered how someone so bright could possibly exist on a day that dark and wet.

"Just like Cooper," she agreed. "We are from the same town. We even went to high school together." Her accent was clearly southern, but not nearly as strong as Cooper's.

"Really?" I asked, not wanting to let the conversation stop.

She smiled wide, and said, "Yessir. But he graduated when I was in the tenth grade."

"Is that how you guys met?" asked Tiffany.

"Gracious, no. I've known Cooper since we was young. He used to work for my Daddy, on our family farm . . ." Cooper cleared his throat—loudly.

Tentatively, Michelle continued, "Can't hardly remember a time in my life when I didn't know Cooper. He was my first love, you know."

"No way," I said. "Cooper never mentioned that."

"Can't say I'm surprised," Michelle said with a hint of mock disappointment. "He's never been one for sharing his feelings." She kicked him under the table. Cooper lowered the menu from his face and blew her a kiss.

"So what brings you to the city?" I asked.

"Well . . . Cooper left Georgia after high school, without so much as a word. No one knew where he got off to—not even me." She looked down at a fat, masculine high school graduation ring, which fit loosely on her thumb. For the first time, in the brief period that I had known her, I saw a crack in her happiness.

Less enthusiastically, she continued, "I lost touch with him until a month ago. I was at college."

Trying to steer the conversation back to something casual and lighthearted, I asked, "College? Really? Which one? For what?"

"University of Georgia," She said. "I'm studying criminal justice."

Honestly curious, I asked, "Criminal justice? No kidding. That's a hard major. What do you want to be?"

"Well . . . you see . . . my mom is a lawyer," Michelle explained. "She works for people who can't afford representation."

Finally deciding to join the conversation, Tiffany said, "That's cool."

Michelle nodded, and continued, "She has even gone to trial . . . for as long as I've been alive, I remember thinking I wanted to be one, too. A lawyer, I mean. Just like my mom. My mom's my idol."

The female bartender came and we ordered our drinks. When the bartender left, to fetch our order, Tiffany asked, "Michelle? Girl, you're a baby. You look like you fifteen. Is you even old enough to buy booze?"

Michelle blushed, and said, "I just turned 21 over the summer."

The four of us were drunk. Tiffany and Cooper had both gone to the bathroom, leaving Michelle and me alone at our table. The bar had accumulated a few patrons, but was still—for the most part—empty.

To a gushing Michelle, I said, "You never told me why you're here in the city." Her mouth snapped shut and she dropped her head comically to the table. I tapped her on her still damp shoulder. "Come on. I want to know."

She hiccupped, lifted her head, and supported it atop both hands. Her fingers smushed her cheeks up, and her eyes disappeared behind narrow slits. When she finally spoke, her words came out in a series of stops and starts. "I. Came. Here. For Cooper."

"What about college?" I asked. "It's still in session, right? Why aren't you there?"

Trying to look serious, she grabbed the, still empty, candleholder, and said, "Hear ye. Hear ye," as she pounded it onto the table, like a makeshift judge's gavel. "I will have order in the court." Her serious face melted, and she again began giggling.

"Honestly," I said. "You want to be a lawyer, right? Can't do that if you're here on vacation."

Her giggling slowed and then stopped. Still supporting her head with her right hand, she started picking at the table with the nails of her left. "Cooper found me online. On the internet." She stopped trying to peel the varnish from the wood, pointed to me, and asked, "You know Facebook, right? That website where people find each other, and post pictures on each other's walls?" I told her that I did, and she continued, "I couldn't believe it. After all these years . . . there he was. He was acting like nothing happened. Like nothing changed." She began picking at the table again. "He told me he lived in Manhattan." She pointed out the door.

"Can you believe it?" she asked. "*My* Cooper in the big city. I almost died when I found out . . . one thing led to another, and then he tells me he is going to buy me a plane ticket . . . how could I refuse? Really . . . how? Who could turn down the big city?" She paused, and looked at me with such sincerity that I had to look away. "Who could turn down their first love?" she asked.

Tiffany and Cooper emerged, from the hallway to the bathroom, together. I was happy to see them both smiling.

Michelle got up from her seat, and said, "I love this song."

Cooper kissed her on the cheek and sat down. She tried to convince him to join her on the dance floor, but he declined adamantly, and she quickly gave up.

Tiffany sat down and dropped the bill on the table. Cooper snatched it before it had a chance to settle, and said, "Fucking hell. Is that it?" He looked presently surprised. "After all we chugged . . . they are only going to charge us for the last two of each of our drinks?" He reached for his wallet. "Tiffany. What the hell are you doing? Blowing the guy?"

Tiffany was watching Michelle dance alone in the middle of the empty floor. "I told you," she said over her shoulder. "He's a fucking customer. Why you so interested? If you want me to give him your phone number, all you have to do is ask."

Cooper was about to lash out at Tiffany when I interjected, "Remember our deal. You pay for two of my drinks."

Visibly annoyed, he looked at me, and said, "That's *all* of your drinks. And . . ." He looked at the bill, then continued, "the shit you got was seven dollars a pop."

I smiled coyly, and said, "Hey man . . . a deal's a deal."

Cooper muttered something under his breath, about how Yankees were bleeding America dry, but I ignored him. Fair was fair, and he owed me two drinks. He pulled, noticeably wet, bills from his wallet and shoved them, and the receipt, toward Tiffany. He looked disgusted, and I could not help but laugh.

Michelle danced to our table and collapsed onto Cooper's lap. Hugging and twisting into him, she whispered loudly, "I dance for you." She repeated herself, over and over, as she began to kiss his neck. "Whenever I dance, I am dancing for you. I'm dancing for you. Being beautiful for you." One of her hands disappeared beneath the waist of his pants.

Cooper moaned for a moment, then barked, "Fuck." He grabbed her wrist and twisted it, up and out of his pants. "Stupid bitch. That hurts."

Suddenly, she was on her knees. Her face contorted in a strange mixture of inebriation and pain. Cooper—now standing—still had her by the wrist and was twisting it. The angle of her hand, in relation to her arm, was so unnatural that I thought her wrist must be broken.

I sat frozen. Not comprehending what I was seeing.

"Please," Michelle howled the word so softly, that I

could hardly hear it. In response, Cooper wrenched her hand even further. "Please. Please, Coop. Don't hurt me, Coop." He held her for a moment longer, and then let her go.

I was ready to stand, and ask her if she was ok, when she shot up from the ground and into Cooper's arms. He stroked her hair as she cried into his chest.

Tiffany and I exchanged nervous looks, and I said, "Hey, Cooper. Tiffany and I have to get going." He did not respond.

Getting to her feet, Tiffany asked, "See you tomorrow at work, Cooper?" His face was buried in Michelle's glowing blonde hair; Cooper nodded, but did not look up.

The air outside of the bar was fresh, and my alcohol dilated nostrils were hungry for the aroma of the night. I sniffed at the world like a dog looking for a bone.

On the verge of once again breaking into giddy laughter, this time at my expense, Tiffany asked, "What are you doing?"

"It smells so clean," I said. "It smells new." Apparently, this made complete sense to Tiffany, who began sniffing too. We sniffed for blocks. Sniffed all the way to my train.

Drunk, and with a slight slur whenever she put emphasis on a word, Tiffany asked, "How did *I* manage to be the one to walk *you* to the train? Isn't that supposed to be the other way around? Ain't it supposed to be the *girl* who gets walked home?"

I looked at her, smiled, and said, "I dunno. We are living in a progressive town; a progressive time." She smiled back at me, and I asked, "Do you want to kiss me?"

She nodded, almost fell over, and said, "I do."

I pointed to my lips, and said, "Go for it."

She closed her eyes and leaned in. At the last moment, I turned and she kissed my cheek. Her lips parted, and a soft, smacking sound tickled my ear.

She leaned back, eyes red and glassy, and through a playful moan said, "You tricked me."

I gave her a hug goodbye, and said, "That's all you get for now."

Chapter 28

While playing with her hair, I asked, "Sofia, do you love me?"

The room was dark, but there was still enough light for my eyes to see. I twisted a soft, brown curl around my finger and let it fall onto her face. The ribbon bounced off of her nose and she stirred.

She turned away from me, and pulled my arm so that it draped across her waist. She made herself small; I made myself big. She wore me like a blanket, and I shielded her from the night.

Before submitting to the blackness of sleep, I whispered, "I love you."

Chapter 29

"Christopher to the manager's office." I could barely hear the announcement over the roaring barrage of angry noises.

The noon rush hour was always bad, but on that day it was terrible. In addition to the normal flood of customers, there were those making up for lost time. Businessmen and women blubbering about the inconvenience of yesterday's rain, and the importance of getting their business sorted *now,* lest their careers end and the world tumble to pieces.

"Christopher to the manager's office," repeated the nearly inaudible announcement.

Tiffany rushed up to me. "Didn't you hear? Eric

wants you in the office."

I pointed to the line of anxious, panic-stricken customers at the consulting table, and said, "This is crazy. How can I leave?"

She grabbed the mouse from my hand and shoved me away from the computer. "Just go," she said, impatiently. "I've got this."

I was about to ask her if she was absolutely sure, when she began consulting the next person in line.

It was a long walk to the office. Not distance long. Spiritually long. Green mile, walking down the hallway to your death, long.

At the very least, I felt like a child who had been summoned by the principal. My chest tightened, and I began to replay the day in my head. Scouring my memory for something that I might have done wrong. Trying to find a reason for the impending reprimand. I could think of nothing, so—conceding to the inevitable—I took a deep breath and knocked on the door. It sprung open immediately, and I braced for the worst.

Eric waved me into the room, and said, "Take a seat."

Take a seat? I thought. *This can't be good.*

The office was small, and barely capable of housing the two chairs that it currently did. Eric was sitting in an office chair and pointed to one made of folding aluminum. I stepped into the room and the heavy door swung and shut solidly behind me.

Paranoia, and an overwhelming feeling of being trapped, filled me. Though I stood calmly, in my mind I was panicking. *This is it.* I thought. *The gas chamber. I am going to die. And I don't even know what I did wrong.*

The room was hot, and thick with body odor. Eric had come to work early that day and spent most of his time in this room. I imagined it being cool in the morning and slowly heating up as his ample girth and heavy, rasping breath slowly heated and changed the uncirculating air to its current temperature and perfume.

Our knees touched as I sat down. "What's up, Eric?" I asked. "Everything good?"

He crossed his right leg over his left, and I was terrified to see the curly, yellow hair of his shin rub sweat into my pants. I tried to shift away, but his leg drooped and rested fully on my knees. I could feel the moisture soak through the fabric and coat my skin.

Eric took a sheet of paper from the small desk, and began to read, "Bachelor's degree in visual arts . . ." He threw the paper back onto the desk, and then he gave me a look, which was both friendly and suspicious.

"Tell me, Christopher," he began. "What are your long-term plans? What are your goals?"

To this I began regurgitating a lie, a lie that I had been honing since before I graduated from college. "I want to be a photographer. It's something I both enjoy and am good at. The reason I am working here is because this is a good stepping-stone . . ."

All of the friendly melted away from his face. He looked at me skeptically, nodded, and said, "Yeah. Perhaps I wasn't making myself clear . . . what are your plans *here*? What are your goals in regards to PaperClips?"

Sensing just how wrong my initial response had been, I backtracked and began damage control. "Well, I am committed to PaperClips. Absolutely, I am. I love the people and I love the work. Nothing satisfies me as much as helping customers fulfill their printing needs. It's really rewarding to me . . . you know?" His response—to what I thought was an obvious, and completely transparent, lie—was a slow nod.

"It's not *exactly* photography," I continued. "But it's close. I get to print posters, and flyers, and even magazines. I'm learning a lot." Look of skepticism unchanged, he nodded again. I was beginning to sweat. The room was hot and my heart was racing. "I don't envision myself leaving any time soon. If that's what you're asking. At least not for a few years . . . This is a stable job . . ." Silent, except for his shallow, hissing breaths, he nodded again. "That isn't to say . . . I mean . . . that's not the only reason I am staying. Just one of the reasons." He nodded, and as he did, a fat bead of sweat rolled down my forehead, then entered and burned my eye.

"I'm learning a lot about printing here," I insisted. "And the work is rewarding. Really rewarding. I'm not going to be leaving anytime soon. I love my job, and the people I work with." I smiled. "And plus you're the best boss I have ever had. Honestly . . . I've had some stinkers in my day. This place is like heaven compared to the pizza place I worked at in college. It was a family-owned place." In an awkward attempt to seem casual and friendly, I tapped him on the knee, and continued, "Can you believe the boss over there actually punched me once? Straight in the arm. Believe it. The boss's father used to come in too. One time, the old man got me in a headlock." I tapped him on the knee again.

I continued, "Yeah. This is heaven compared to that place. . . . Even not compared to that place this place is still really good." He nodded.

I was running out of things to say. "The work is really rewarding." I repeated. "I love the work."

He started slowly. "You may not realize this . . ." he leaned forward in his chair. "But I have been watching you."

He pointed to the computer on the desk. "For about a month now I have been watching you. Remember how I told you we have cameras and mics throughout the store?"

I was about to say that I remembered when he cut me off. "I've been watching the cameras and I have to say that I am impressed, Chris. You don't get flustered. You get your work done on time. All the staff seem to like you. Especially Tiffany." I said that Tiffany was a good worker and a nice person. That it was a pleasure to work with someone as professional as her.

He agreed, then said, "As you know Tiffany is my star worker." He pointed a fat scaly finger in my direction. "So, when she recommends someone for promotion, I tend to listen."

Not knowing what to say, I began to stutter and mumble, something like: "I don't . . . I . . . I . . . uh . . . understand . . . maybe . . ."

"Don't be surprised," he said, with a condescending

smirk. "This has actually been in the works for a long time. Since before we even hired you, in fact." He pointed a finger through the wall to the production area. "Maria . . . she's just not *working out*. Hasn't been working out for a while. She's slow. She gets flustered. She always stays *late*." He said "late" with a growl, and as he did his face turned a deep shade of red.

He paused, grabbed a can of energy drink from the table, and, after a long gulp, continued. "It is just not working. Production is a mess. We need someone who knows how to prioritize. We need someone who works through the mess, and gets the job done. We need someone who gets the job done, *AND* leaves on time. We need a new Production Expert. I think that should be you."

I did not know why, but I suddenly had to fart— and loudly. Clinching my cheeks and shifting, uncomfortably, in my seat, I managed a hesitant, "I don't know what to say."

Eric took another sip of his drink, then said, "We were actually considering borrowing a Production Expert from another store to replace Maria. But only as a last resort. Here, at PaperClips, we prefer to promote from within." He gave me a wink. "Either way, she's gone. If you agree I'm going to tell her to train you for Production Expert. She'll train you up and when she's done . . ." He snapped his fingers so loudly that the sound echoed within the small room. Startled, by the power and suddenness of the noise, my clenching relaxed for an instant. A small puff of air escaped silently from between my cheeks. I smiled toothily, and he continued, "you'll replace her." He extended a hand. "What do you say? This is a big opportunity, Chris. And a big pay bump. Are you up for it?"

I smiled a wide, fake smile, shook his hand, and enthusiastically said, "Of course I am."

"Okay. Good. I want this to happen as soon as possible, so I'm going to have you stay late today. All right? Stay over into the next shift so that Maria can begin coaching you." I told him that it would be no problem for me to stay late and left the office.

The door clicked shut behind me, and I let it rip. The fart was huge, but silent. *Maybe, I should cut back on the drinking.* I thought absently, as I walked to the front. *Maybe, just quit beer. All those bubbles are making me gassy. Yeah, from now on, I should try and stick to wine, and liquor.*

"You fired?" asked Tiffany when I went to the front. The line to the consulting table was gone and now only a few customers wandered the aisles.

"No," I said, touching my cold hands to my fire-hot face.

"You're all red."

I flipped my hands over and pressed their cool backsides against my cheeks. Trying to speak normally, despite my rapidly beating heart, I said, "It is hot in the office."

"You were in there for a long time. What happened? You get in trouble? *Break any rules?*" she asked. I looked at her and was surprised to see that she seemed nervous.

"No, nothing like that. No. Not at all. I'm up for a promotion. Production Expert."

"Congratulations, bitch," she said, and slapped me on the shoulder.

"Yeah. Maria is going to start training me today."

"Shit. Eric moves quick. Can't say I'm surprised. Dude hates Maria. Has forever. In fact . . . shit, I'm surprised he kept her around this long."

"Why did he?" I asked. "I mean if he hated her so much, why keep her around?"

"He just didn't want to fire her. Brings down our numbers or something." She grabbed her purse from under the register and plucked out a pack of cigarettes and a pink lighter. Then she stuck them between her breasts, and said, "Something corporate, I guess. Makes the store look bad."

"Then why is he doing it now?"

She adjusted her shirt, and it was impossible to tell that she had anything hidden beneath it. The paraphernalia was buried so deep that I wondered if she'd ever be able to find the objects again. "Guess he's just tired of it. She always stays late. He always be gettin' written up because of it . . . She makes him look bad *now*. Guess he doesn't care if firing her makes her look bad in the future."

When it was time to clock out, I took my lunch break instead. I could not leave, but I did walk Cooper and Tiffany out, and lingered with them in front of the store while Tiffany smoked a cigarette.

"Can't hardly believe they're making your sheepish ass the boss," bitched Cooper. "I've got more leadership ability in my baby toe than you got in your whole damn body."

He kicked a soda can and it shot down the sidewalk, jumped the curb, and bounced out onto the street. "There's no justice in the world," Cooper said, solemnly. "No, sir. It ain't right. I just might have to quit . . . on principle."

"Will you *'quit'* whining like a little bitch?" Tiffany laughed the question, as she exhaled a cloud of gray.

Cooper stiffened visibly. "Who the fuck's whining?" He looked at me, and in an acerbic tone asked, "Do you hear anyone whining, Chris?" I shrugged and laughed a little at his expense.

Cooper stepped towards Tiffany. "Who the fuck's whining?" he asked. Each word sounding progressively angrier than the last.

She ignored him, smiled faintly, and then sucked on her cigarette. This time she exhaled through her nose. Her nostrils flared and smoke shot out in two perfect jets. She reminded me of a cartoon bull: playfully angry and ready to charge.

Cooper stepped closer to Tiffany. He was posturing aggressively, but she seemed amused. Not, in the least bit, scared.

Again, he stepped toward Tiffany. They were so close now that it looked as though they were lovers. At that distance it did not look like Cooper was getting ready to fight. At that distance it looked like Cooper was leaning in for a kiss. "I wasn't whining." His lips grew thin and exposed his teeth as he spoke. "I'm happy for Chris. I'm just not sure Eric is making the best choice."

He paused for a moment, and then leaned in close to her ear. Cooper looked like a man about to whisper a secret. But the words that came out of his mouth were no softer then the ones he had just spoken. "I just can't help but wonder . . . if someone is playing favorites."

She pushed him away. He tripped and staggered back across the sidewalk. Tiffany and I both laughed as Cooper fell into a pile of trash and cardboard boxes marked for recycling. "That's what you get," said Tiffany, with a smile that spanned the width of her face.

At once Cooper was back on his feet and charging. I was about to step between them when . . . "Tiffany. What up baby? I came to walk you home like old times."

Vinny stepped in, between them, and extended an arm in my direction. I bumped his fist with mine and he gave Tiffany a kiss. She opened her mouth wide, to accommodate his tongue, but his tongue did not come. His mouth was closed, and his dry kiss landed awkwardly on her top lip.

I was not sure how much he had seen. But it was clear that he had seen something. Because Vinny regarded Cooper coldly. Vinny, who obviously worked out at a gym, was both taller and heavier than Cooper. A tense moment passed as they stared at each other.

Finally, Vinny turned to me and asked, "Who is this joker?"

"This is Cooper. He works with us in the mornings," I replied.

Vinny's words developed a strangely pointed quality that made each syllable sound like an accusation. "That right? So, you're the *other guy* who works with my girl Tiffany. Well, excuse me if I don't shake your hand, *Coop*.

Looks like it's covered in dog shit."

We all looked at Cooper's hand. It was covered in something brown and wet. He brought it to his nose and sniffed it. "It's chocolate," he said.

"Yeah, well . . . excuse me anyway," Vinny said, as he turned to Tiffany. He put his hand into her back pocket and squeezed. "Ready to go, you sexy bitch?"

"See you guys tomorrow," she said, looking at me with apologetic eyes. She threw down her cigarette, and her eyes darted to Cooper. "Try and be on time for once."

Cooper made a fist. I could hear the "chocolate" squish between his fingers.

Before rounding the corner, and disappearing from view, Vinny looked back at Cooper.

Eric called me into his office when my lunch was over. The room was even hotter now. Not quite a sauna, but close. I had to stand, as a gently weeping Maria occupied the extra chair.

Eric picked an orange crumb from the corner of his mouth, ate it, then said, "I talked to Maria about the situation. She's *agreed* to give me her two weeks notice, and train you in the allotted time." I looked at Maria. Her gentle sobs peaked, but she was obviously holding back. Her look said she wanted to be bawling.

"Okay," Eric said, and turned his chair. He slapped the keyboard, and the computer woke from its sleep. A grid of real-time surveillance videos, being shot from high angles, emerged from behind the screensaver. I could see the entire store, and people—like ants—walking within it.

He put on a pair of greasy headphones, which had tattered and frayed foam cushions on the speakers, and continued. "I want you guys to start immediately." He pointed to Maria without looking at her. "Maria. Train your replacement."

When we left the office, Maria excused herself and went to the bathroom. I waited outside the door. Inside, I could hear sobs and the sound of a nose being blown. After a long moment she emerged, wet and red.

"Follow me to the back," she said, wiping her eyes with her shoulders. "I'm going to show you how to order toners, fusers, and drums for the Xerox machines."

We were halfway there when a voice screeched over the intercom, "Maria to the consulting table." She made a beeline to the front, and I followed her.

The customer was an old woman. Her hands shook violently as she handed Maria an old, cracked photograph. The image—once black and white—had turned yellow with age. As Maria examined it so did I.

It was a picture of a beautiful, blonde woman holding a plump, smiling child. The child—who was holding another child, in the form of a rag doll—had obviously moved during the long exposure. Her dress and arms were crisply in focus. But her feet and face were blurred. Regardless of the motion blur, her smile was still unmistakable.

"That's me and my mother," the woman told Maria, in a raspy voice that popped with every other word.

Maria's tears were gone, and she seemed to brighten

at hearing the woman's voice. "And what would you like to have done today?" she asked, as perky as ever.

"Well . . . my grandson came to visit me the other day, and we got to talking about family history." She pointed a thin, vibrating finger—with bulging arthritic joints—at the picture. "We were going through an old album together when I found that." She dropped her finger and motioned to the consulting table's computer. "He commented on how it was fading, and told me that I should get a digital copy made."

She looked at Maria with mock shame, and said, "I suppose, I could have done this at home. He bought me a computer and a printer-scanner combo last year . . . so that we can keep in touch through email . . . but I never did get the hang of that awful machine." She motioned again to the computer. "Someone told me you scan images here. Is that true?"

"Absolutely," said Maria. "I'll be right back." Maria disappeared into the back with the image and reemerged less then a minute later. "Okay," she said as she called up the image on the computer. "Let's see what we can do."

This was a straightforward job. Scan and email. Nothing complicated. It should have taken less than five minutes, but we stood at that table for forty-five. Maria had a long, warm conversation with the woman, while she digitally restored the color and removed the cracks.

We were capable of doing this kind of restoration, but only when it was explicitly requested. And even then, only at the steep base price of thirty dollars. A price the customer was required to approve before we even began the work.

Maria did not mention the fee.

If we did end up taking in a digital job, we usually sent it off to a third party design service. As a rule we tried to do as little digital work in-house as possible. The reason for this was two-fold. It took *a lot* of time and, aside from Maria and myself, no one knew how to do it. This was a perfect illustration of that fact. Forty-five minutes, for nothing. Luckily no line of customers demanding our help had yet formed. But I reasoned it was only a matter of time. Especially if Maria took this long with every customer who walked through the door.

"Maria," I said softly, not wanting the customer to hear. "I think we should move on. There is a lot you still need to show me and this is taking a lot longer than . . ." She gave me a look that said I had better stop talking, and be quiet. I did.

Standing there watching Maria interact with the customer, and retouch the photo with the care and delibera-tion of someone restoring a Rembrandt painting, something dawned on me. Maria took her job seriously. More than that, Maria cared!

She cared about PaperClips in a way that I never could. Earlier that day, when I lied to Eric about how I found the work to be satisfying and fulfilling, I could not imagine anyone honestly feeling that way. Yet, here she was.

This was more than a job to Maria. This was her life. She did not stay late because she wanted the extra hours. She stayed late because . . . she liked the work. Amazingly, she liked the work, and she liked working at

PaperClips.

People hated her for all the wrong reasons. She was not slow because she was trying to make more money from overtime. She was not slow because she wanted to sabotage the group. She took her time because she treated customers like people, instead of commodities, and that connection took time. She took her time, because doing good work took time. She worked slowly, because she took pride in her work and she wanted to do it right.

Suddenly, I felt bad for Maria.

I left work that day with a new perspective, and with a lot of serious questions. Why was *I* being promoted? I did not care about this job in the least. Yet, I was being chosen to replace the one person in the whole world who did? Why? Because she worked too hard, and because nobody liked her? Because everyone liked me? Because *Tiffany* liked me? It did not seem right.

Chapter 30

I had been checking my apartment's mailbox, and my computer's email inbox, compulsively. Twice, sometimes three times a day, I would rush down to the mailbox. Even on Sundays.

It was not rational. Mail came once a day and never on Sundays, but I could not help myself. I was expecting news. Life affirming or devastating, it did not matter. I wanted to know as soon as possible. Was I to become a published author, or was I just a fool who dared to hope?

I had just come back from my first check of the day, and was sitting down on the couch to read when someone knocked at the door. I jumped from the couch, dropping *Catch-22* onto the floor in the process, and sprinted toward the sound.

This is it, I thought. *Finally. News. I don't know why I was looking in my mailbox. This is the big leagues. This is probably the company courier, with an edited copy of my novel and a check.*

I ripped the door open expecting the best and . . . I was sorely disappointed.

"What up, fag?" Cooper asked, and handed me a heavy paper bag. "Ready to get wasted?" He pushed past me and entered my apartment. "Hasn't changed since the last time I was here. When the hell you going to decorate? If it wasn't for all these books scattered everywhere the place would look like a damned crack house."

I went to the kitchen and unloaded the bag. Three bottles of red wine and a fifth of cheap whisky. "The wine is for you," Cooper said with a raspy chuckle. "Since I know you're a pretty lady who loves wine." He pulled up the hems of an invisible dress and curtsied. In response I presented him with a one-fingered salute.

"That's not right, sweetie," he said, still chuckling. "What will the kids think?" Cooper grabbed, unscrewed, and drank from the whisky bottle. Three deep gulps.

I put two bottles of wine in the freezer, uncorked the third, and asked, "Why are you here?"

"What? Why so damn cold? Can't I get no love? Shit. Just brought you three bottles of red." He paused to take another gulp, and then continued, "Not even a thank you?"

He had brought the wine and I was thankful for that. I suddenly felt bad that I had not said so sooner.

"Thanks, Cooper."

It was not often people came bearing unsolicited alcoholic drinks. In point of fact, I could remember more than a few times I had had to resort to begging.

"No problem," he said.

I watched as Cooper wobbled his way to the cabinet above the sink. He opened it and grabbed a glass from the front. It was then that I realized something . . . . It was eleven in the morning, and this yokel was already drunk.

"Why are you here?" I asked between long sips of wine.

"What? A guy can't show up at his friend's house for a few drinks?"

"Sure you can . . . but you never do," I insisted. "What's the occasion?"

He picked the glass up and held it in front of his thinly drawn, bloodshot eyes. Cooper studied the glass for a moment then asked, "Where'd you get this?"

"That's my Tom and Jerry jelly jar glass," I said with more than a dash of pride. "I used to have a lot more of them, but they all got broken. That's my last one."

Still studying it, he said, "I used to have the same thing when I was a kid. My family had a whole collection. The whole set. I used to love them. Little cartoons on the glass . . . made me feel fancy. Like we had money and could afford the nice things." He placed the glass back into the cupboard, then pulled out a green plastic cup. He filled the cup halfway with whisky, the rest of the way with water, then took a sip.

I sniffed at the rim of my wine bottle, then kissed it,

slow and deep. The liquid was warm and coated my tongue and insides as I drank. A familiar feeling that brought a deep calm over me.

"Come on," I said, while catching my breath. "Let's go sit in the living room. I'll put on some music to drink to."

I set my laptop up to play some country music. Old stuff. The kind of country music where the steel guitar screams, and the deep voice singing sounds like it belongs to a man who is on the verge of tears.

When I joined Cooper in the living room, he was holding a book. It was the book that, in my haste to answer the door, I had dropped next to the couch. Not reading the book, but experiencing it, he flipped back and forth through the pages and sniffed at the breeze they made. He opened to the center of the book and buried his nose into the fold. He took a number of deep, noisy inhales. As I came closer he stopped and seemed to judge its weight in his hand.

"I never read this book," he said. "Is it any good?"

"I just started it," I said, as I sat down and relaxed into the worn black leather of the hand-me-down sofa. "I heard it got banned for having 'dangerous' language. So, naturally, I had to read it."

"Dangerous language?" Cooper asked. "The hell you mean by that?"

"I don't know," I said. "I guess it has a lot of swears."

Cooper gave me a look of honest surprise, and said, "How's cussing dangerous language?"

"I don't know, man. You should ask the people of Ohio. I read they banned it in the seventies."

"Banned *Catch-22*?" he asked. "But, ain't this book a classic? Don't they make you read it in school or something?"

"Not in the school I went to," I said, taking another sip of my wine.

He threw the book across the room, and it landed in the corner atop a pile of clothes. I thought about yelling at him, but figured it was not worth the trouble. He was drunk, and I was well on my way to joining him.

Cooper looked at his hands, ripped off a flap of dried, dead skin from his left palm, and said, "I had to get out of my apartment. Michelle won't get off my back."

"About what?" I asked, taking another swig of wine from the almost-empty bottle.

"She wants me to move back down south. Wants me to live with her down there. She says I'm not doing anything with my life up here."

"Do you think you are?" I asked. "I mean . . . do you . . ."

"Shut up. I know what you mean. Shit, it's all I ever think about. Honestly . . . ? I dunno. I thought so. I thought I was doing something. I thought I had a plan. But PaperClips has a way of draining a man. I go in early and work all day. When I get out, the day's still young, but I'm dog-tired. I work, sleep, drink, and work. I don't do nothing else. I don't have the energy."

"I understand," I said, solemnly.

I did. Truly, I did. I understood completely.

Cooper sipped his drink, and said, "I thought this was the land of opportunity . . . I'm not so sure anymore."

A moment of silence passed between us, and then I got up to get another bottle. When I returned he had a distant look. His was the face of someone in deep thought, or that of someone dreaming with his eyes open.

I passed him and Cooper blinked heavily. "No," he said. "I worked too hard to get to where I am. It may not seem like much, but I am the most successful person in my family. I'm proud of that. I worked hard to get here and I'm not going to leave." He paused for a long time, and I let the silence ring. "It just seems too much like giving up. Like, if I move back it proves that I'm no better than the rest. Just . . . just another loser. Just another piece of white trash. I can't take that. I can't."

Chapter 31

As usual, Cooper was late for work. Normally Tiffany and I would have gone inside the store and prepared to open up shop, but today we waited outside. The morning air was crisp, and easy to breathe. It whipped down my throat and chilled my body from the inside out. Chilled me in a way that made me feel fresh, and clean, and alive.

Neither of us wanted to go inside. Neither of us wanted to start the day. Savoring those last precious moments as individuals, before we went into the store and became employees, we leaned against the base of that 59th Street skyscraper, and talked.

Tiffany pounded an unopened pack of cigarettes against her palm, and asked, "What do you mean you're not sure?"

I shook my head, and said, "I always thought this was temporary. Like, that I would work here just long enough to get established. Or . . . until I found a better job . . . not make this my career."

Her look said she had heard this kind of thing before and was not interested in pandering to me. To this I took offense.

"Listen," I began. "I mean, how can I be happy here? How can *you* be happy here? How can anybody? It doesn't contribute anything to your life besides a paycheck . . . and mine's not even that big." I paused, listened to the slapping noise, and wondered just how much pounding a new pack of cigarettes required.

"Every day here, it's the same thing," I said, while my eyes stayed hypnotically locked on to the bouncing pack. "Over and over. You can't get a leg up, even if you tried. If you finish everything one day, a fresh load of the same shit will come in the next. Every day the workload resets. A new pile of shit waiting for me in the production area. I mean . . . I'm just sick of shoveling shit all day." Finally, she unwrapped the pack, pinched out a stick and lit it up.

Still trying to make her see my point of view, I continued. "I feel like I'm running in place. And, it's making me nervous." I thumped my chest with the side of a loose fist. "Like, in my heart. I feel it all of the time. It wouldn't be so bad, if this was a PaperClips in the country. A place where we had one customer a day. But this place is killing me. Get everything done, and get it done right away.

Frantically shuffle. Frantically juggle. Frantically finish. Frantically finish nothing."

She smiled and shook her head, like a parent listening to a child. A child who is trying to talk about a subject of which they have no real understanding.

I slid down the building's cold steel façade, and landed in a crouched position. With a sigh, I asked, "Don't you want anything more?"

"Like you said Chris: it's a paycheck. . . ." She took a drag of her cigarette, then continued. "Don't get it twisted, though. I'ma get out of here eventually. I don't see myself here in five years. But this is good enough for now. And besides, I make more than you. My paycheck satisfies me just fine."

I looked up at her and said, "I just get scared for my future. You know? Seems so easy to get trapped. Like every day I spend here is a day I don't spend making my life better. And, eventually, it will be too late."

"We're young," she said, as she used the cherry from the first cigarette to light a second. "Don't stress it. We got plenty of time."

"I've been saying that for years, Tiffany. And, to tell you the truth . . . I don't feel so young anymore."

Cooper was running later than usual. Normally, he ambled into work no later than an hour past his scheduled start time. Here it was, eleven in the morning, and he was still nowhere to be seen.

Despite his lateness, we figured he would be into work eventually. Because, if he was skipping—which he did often—we would have gotten the obligatory message saying that he was sick, or in the throes of a family emergency, or both.

I was just about to call him when Cooper walked through the door. His hair was a mess and he was wearing the same clothes as the day before. As he approached, I could smell whisky on his breath, and I wondered if he had gone to bed after leaving my house or simply continued to drink.

I followed him back to the break room, and said, "You look like shit, man."

He turned to me sharply, and exploded, "Don't you fuck with me today, Chris. I'm not in the mood."

I stood my ground, and said, "Shit, man, chill. What? Are you still drunk?"

He turned away and pulled his uniform from a locker. "Yeah, I woke up drunk, and with a five-alarm hangover," Cooper said, as he pulled the black pants up and over his jeans. The result of this layering was legs that looked thick with tumors. Adjusting his crotch, he continued, "I woke up drunk and sick, so I drank more whisky to feel better." I nodded that I understood. In fact, I had done the same thing. But, instead of whisky, I drank two tall cans of beer.

He pulled the PaperClips shirt over his hooded sweatshirt. Now, he looked like a homeless person layered in found clothes. One who had stumbled across a Paper-Clips uniform in a trash bin somewhere. "I spent the last three hours feeling like shit and choking down whisky," he said, then paused to burp. "And, to make things worse, I couldn't stop fighting with Michelle."

"What's wrong now?" I asked, fanning the whisky smell away from my nose.

"Same shit as before. She won't drop it. She's convinced moving back is the thing to do. I can't talk her out of it. Bitch is stubborn." He punched the locker so hard that it left a dent. "She told me she bought a plane ticket last night, while I was at your house. Says she's got to get back to school. Back to her fucking family. Says she is going tonight with or without me."

"So what are you going to do?"

"What the fuck you think, Chris? I can't go back there. Nothing for me back there."

"What about Michelle?" I asked.

Despite the sadness in his eyes, he said, "Fuck her."

There was an unusual amount of tension in the air that day. A static charge that made my skin tingle, and the short hairs on the back of my neck stand at attention. It felt like a storm was coming, but outside the sky was blue, and the only thunder was the boom of Cooper's voice as he treated customers poorly.

The day continued like this. I expected something to happen. I envisioned a customer confronting Cooper about his poor customer-service skills. In my mind I saw Cooper flying into a rage. I imagined him ripping a register from the counter and beating a businessman with it for asking if we "make copies." I waited with perverted eagerness for him to assault someone. Waited for him to break the tension and ever-present monotony of that day.

Cooper was rude, and gave the minimum, but I could tell he was holding back. The drink from this morning had granted him a measure of self-control. But, for how long? How long until the drink wore off, or the thinly veiled fury overpowered its liquid jailer? It was like working with a bomb. An explosion was coming. It seemed inevitable.

In the back, Tiffany looked up from her phone, and asked, "The fuck's Cooper's problem today?" Her phone buzzed in her hand, and she looked back down at it. Then she began typing.

"Michelle is leaving him," I explained.

"Good," Tiffany said, coldly. "That bitch deserves better than his ass. Anyone can tell he don't treat her right. Besides, she's motivated. She's going places." She shook her head, and I detected more happiness than pity in her voice. "Cooper's not going anywhere."

"Why do you say that?" I asked, a little surprised by her candor.

She looked up from her phone again. "Just look at him. Nigga's crazy. Stupid bitch is gunna end up killing someone one of these days. Dude ain't headed nowhere but prison."

I felt a sudden and irrational need to defend Cooper. "Do you ever get tired of speaking like that?" I asked.

Still looking down at her phone, she asked, "Like how?"

"Bitch, nigga, ain't . . . why don't you just speak English?"

She looked up and smiled cautiously. She was trying to discern if I was joking. Then, apparently deciding that, yes, I was indeed joking, her smile slowly widened, and she said, "Listen, not everyone has to talk like you, Mr. Man."

"It's not even about that," I said harshly. "It's about communicating. Saying what you mean in a way that people can understand."

"The fuck?" she asked, and slammed her phone on-to the counter.

"It doesn't even sound believable," I said. "Sounds fake."

"Oh what, and you sound real?" she asked. She stood, adjusted imaginary glasses, and began to read from an invisible book. "I umm. Gosh be darned. Would you look at the economy? The state of affairs in this country today . . ." She slammed shut the invisible book and tossed it onto the counter next to her phone.

She put one hand on her hip, and pointed at me with the other. "I remember a time before rap music when America was a good and safe place," she said. "Before the *blacks* got their hands on it. Now its *nigger this* and *bitch that*." She shuddered as she swore. As if the words were so bad their very mention gave her chills. "I miss the good old days, when a gallon of milk only cost a nickel."

"It's not about that," I repeated. "It's not about race. It's about speaking clearly. Using the right words." She stared at me. I stared back. "It is NOT about race," I insisted. "There are plenty of black people who speak properly, and plenty of white people who don't. Cooper, for example. Sometimes, I can't understand what he is saying. Just like, sometimes, I can't understand you. Don't you want me to understand you? Isn't that the point of speaking? Why wouldn't you try and make it as easy for me to understand your meaning as possible? Why would you fuck with that? There is enough misunderstanding in the world. You don't need to make it worse by not speaking clearly."

"You know what?" she asked. "When you first started here I thought you was faking the way you talk." I must have looked surprised because she nodded enthusiastically, as if responding to something I had said. "Yeah. Believe it. I thought you were trying to sound intelligent. Trying to impress everyone with your big-ass vocabulary."

Insulted, I asked, "What? I would never try . . ."

She cut me off. "The more I got to know you the more I realized you were just a fucking snob. You never said anything, but I always knew you felt superior."

"I don't . . ."

She cut me off again. "Super smart Christopher is too good for PaperClips. He's too good to be manager. Even that's beneath him . . . didn't you know? He's going to be somebody. He is going to make something of himself. He's going to change the whole fucking world." She wiped spit from the corner of her mouth. "Well, I've got news for you—you smug sonofabitch—you *ain't* doing shit. Nothing. Not a damn thing. You're here with all the rest of us simple folk."

She turned and left the break room. Crossing the threshold, she spoke over her shoulder, "Guess that makes you simple too, huh?"

Her words stung. I had not thought of myself as being pretentious, but I supposed that I had been. I had never been someone who was humble. And, I had always considered that to be a strength. One of the reasons I went to school and graduated. One of the reasons I moved to the city. I always told everyone how amazing and smart I was, and, in the end, that turned into a sort of self-fulfilling prophecy.

Me: "I'm so smart."

The World: "Oh yeah? Let's see you graduate from high school."

Me: "Did it. See? Told you I was smart."

The World: "Oh yeah? Why don't you go to college?"

Me: "Okay, I will."

The World: "Get a degree that proves just how special you really are. If you can."

Me: "Done. Not only am I super smart, but now I realize that I am talented to boot."

The World: "Oh yeah? Why don't you move to the city and prove it?"

Me: "Ok, I will."

The World: "How are you going to pay for rent?"

Me: "I'll work at PaperClips until I'm discovered as being a genius. That should only take a few days."

A few days turned into a few months, and now here

I was, standing in the PaperClips break room, wondering if I had been lying to myself, and the world, all along.

I followed Tiffany out of the store. She lit a cigarette and leaned against the building, seemingly exhausted.

I smiled at her.

"Don't give me that smile, Chris. You give that fake-ass smile all day, to everyone. Every customer, and every one of your coworkers. I'm sick of it. Don't give it to me. Don't give it to me now. Don't give it to me ever."

"It's not fake," I said, as I stretched the smile wider.

"Who the fuck do you think you're lying to? I've seen your smile and that thing you're wearing on your face ain't it. That's the uniform. And let me tell you what, Chris. You wear it badly."

I had wronged Tiffany, and for that I felt horrid.

"I'm sorry," I said. "You are right." I dropped the smile, and dropped my eyes to the ground. "I am a pretentious asshole." I couldn't look at her. The anger and hurt in her eyes was too much for me to bear. "I'm pretentious, and I lashed out at you because I'm beginning to realize . . . that . . . well . . . I'm beginning to realize that I'm no better than anyone else. Shit. I'm beginning to realize that I'm worse. I'm a douche bag. The worst kind of douche bag. I'm a douche bag with pretentions."

The truth of my words hit me hard. My eyes began to burn with tears. My chin trembled. It was midday, on a Manhattan sidewalk. I should have been ashamed of myself for crying in public, but I was not. I felt so much shame at this point that any more would have gone unnoticed.

Tiffany hugged me. I let myself be hugged.

"I'm sorry," I said.

"Me too," she replied. "If it makes you feel any better, I think you *are* the smartest nigger I know."

"Thanks," I said, weeping into her shoulder.

Chapter 32

"Do you feel better, you weepy, little bitch?"

"What are you talking about?" I asked, already knowing the answer to my question.

"I saw you with Tiffany."

I avoided looking at Cooper. "What do you mean? I don't know what you are talking about," I lied.

"Ah, come on. Don't give me that. You two left me with a store full of customers . . . I was pissed. I was about to go outside, and give you both a piece of my mind, when I saw your bitch ass crying like a ten-year-old girl. Highlight of my fucking day. Nearly shit myself, I laughed so hard." He punched me in the arm. "That's for making me laugh so hard when I have a hangover."

"Whatever," I said.

"Come on. Don't worry. I won't tell anyone." There was something unfamiliar about his words. They sounded sincere. Almost kind. He continued, "I've always believed that it's okay for a man to cry. So long as he's got a reason; I don't see no problem with it." He punched me again, but softer. "Tell you the truth, I cry all the time. It's therapeutic. Gets the bad out of you. It's good for the heart."

I was surprised by this. I thought Cooper was a lot of things; emotionally aware was not among them.

"Still hungover?" I asked. "How do you feel? Still sick?"

Cooper shrugged. "Nah. The hangover is gone. I'm drunk though. Been drinking all day."

"Really?" I asked, with a laugh. "At work?"

"Where else?"

"They have cameras. You know that right? They can definitely fire you for drinking on the job."

"So?" he asked, in a defiant tone.

"You're crazy, Cooper."

He smiled, and looked proud to be labeled thus. "Thanks, bud," he said, "You know, I hate to tell you this, but you ain't exactly a model of mental health yourself."

I shook my head and laughed. And, the laughter felt good. Cooper may have been crazy. He may even have been a violent and potentially dangerous man. But he was also my friend. A fact that I had taken for granted.

This time, I punched him. Not hard, but hard enough. "I'm sorry to hear about Michelle. She's a good woman. I know how much she means to you." He nodded solemnly, but did not respond. "I want you to know . . . I am here if you need me. If you need anything, don't hesitate to ask."

"Quit being gay." He looked at me thankfully, and smiled.

I smiled back, and said, "Fair enough."

The subway was busy. It was three in the afternoon, and in addition to workers fresh off of the job, there were legions of children. Each and every one of them were: loud, awkward, anxious, full of life, and without an outlet. Restless. Nothing to do, and nowhere to go besides a subway car.

I could hardly hear Cooper over the cacophony of pubescent bickering. "Wanna go to the bar by my house?"

"The Piper's Kilt?" I asked.

"Where else? It's the only good pub in Inwood."

"We could go to Mamajuana's," I offered.

"And, do what?" Cooper asked, with a scowl. "Order a fruity Sangria?"

"I dunno. Maybe."

"Eww," he said, as he backed away, arms held up in front of him in a defensive position. "I knew it. You love the cock."

"No. I just thought we could go someplace new. Try and break our routines."

"Whatever. So long as they have beer, and liquor,

and . . ."

"Hey. You. Hey. Hey." The words came fast and in rapid succession. They cut Cooper off, midsentence. It was Vinny, and he was charging through the crowd in our direction.

Cooper elbowed me, and spoke as quietly as he could while still being heard. "Look who it is. Think he knows about you and Tiffany?"

I did not know, but his stride made me doubt this was going to be a pleasant conversation. As he came closer I stiffened, and prepared to fight.

"You," Vinny pointed in our direction. "I want to talk to you." He screamed the words.

The closer he came, the faster he walked. Until he was finally running. I made fists and bent my knees. Childhood fights had taught me to keep a low center of gravity. It made it easier to maneuver. It made it easier to stay on your feet.

He was on us in seconds. I braced my self for a blow, and was surprised to see Vinny plow headlong into Cooper's chest.

Cooper careened into the side of a chrome newsstand. The sound of meat slapping metal rang loudly, and echoed throughout the 59th Street station.

Cooper was trying to get to his feet, when Vinny grabbed him by the collar of his shirt. He dragged Cooper towards his fist, then punched him in the face.

Cooper looked confused as Vinny punched him again, and yelled, "Fucking my girl." Another punch. "You piece of shit." Another punch. And, another. Cooper coughed, and blood flew from his nose and mouth, onto Vinny's fist, as he punched him again. "Thought I wouldn't find out? Didn't you? But, I knew. I knew all along."

Then, something changed in Cooper. Hate and fury ate the look of confusion, and he was back on his feet. Vinny swung and punched Cooper in the eye. I could almost see the skin rip. Blood began to flow.

Cooper, unfazed by his bleeding mouth, nose, and eye, lunged at his opponent. A flurry of fists, and kicking feet. Vinny tried to block the assault, but the attacks came fast and solid. Vinny backed away, and Cooper followed. Kicking and punching.

By now, a circle of hecklers had formed around the two. Most cheered, some gasped, but no one intervened. Not even me.

Cooper began to scream. No words. Just noise. A deep, primal sound.

Vinny—trying to regain dominance—punched with a series of slow, heavy blows to Cooper's chest. Each connection sounded like a wooden bat hitting a soft pillow. Cooper began to wheeze, but never slowed his assault.

Slowly, Cooper's wheezing morphed in to a mad laughter, and he began punching even faster. The blows, up until this point, had been uncalculated, landing randomly. Now they seemed focused. Each, and every one of Cooper's blow landed someplace vital. The eyes. The nose. The mouth. The neck.

Cooper landed a solid blow on the bobbing bulge in the front of Vinny's throat. Unable to breath, Vinny stopped punching and clasped his neck with both hands.

He looked surprised, and scared. Terrified even.

The previously confident, strangely charismatic man now looked like a frightened child. A youth experiencing an apocalyptic pain. A pain which he had never even dared to imagine.

He reeled back and lifted one hand from his neck and extended it in front of his face in defense. He squeezed his eyes closed, and backed away blindly. Further, and further, and further.

Cooper, perhaps sensing that he had won, stopped his attack and stood watching, as Vinny backed away in terror; gasping for air with every step.

Gagging, wheezing, coughing, and choking Vinny continued to stagger backwards. He continued backwards despite the cries of warning. Despite the screams.

I could hear the train coming, and when Vinny fell onto the tracks, I knew, with a cold certainty, that he was going to die.

Chapter 33

The taxi ride home was long. Made longer still by the fact that I could not stop thinking about what had happened. Those last fatal seconds of screaming, screeching metal, and the wet crunch that had followed.

Cooper ran away after the fight. I did not know where he was, or what he was doing. I imagined him bleeding in a jail cell somewhere. I imagined him crying, and reflecting on his now ruined life. Reflecting on the bitter realization that whatever dreams he may have had were now just that: dreams.

Sitting there, in a state of mild shock, it dawned on me just how similar we actually were. We had the same goal: to be something.

We both wanted to improve our situation. We both wanted to show the world—all those who had doubted us—just how much we could achieve. We both had the same foolish pride. The same unjustified sense of self worth.

Both our paths had led us to the city. Had led us to PaperClips. We even lived in the same neighborhood. He beat his girlfriend, and I was planning to cheat on mine.

The taxi driver asked, "Where you say? Two-oh-seven and what?"

"Broadway," I said, nervously folding my hands into each other. "I'm going to the Piper's Kilt."

He fell silent and continued to our destination. I was glad he was not a talkative cabby. In my state, I could not have handled a conversation.

When we reached our destination, I handed the cabby his money, and exited the vehicle. He had dropped me off at the door. If I had realized it sooner, I would have given him a tip.

I should have gone home, but I decided, as soon as I was away from the crowd of screaming commuters, that I needed a beer. I chose the Piper's Kilt because it was fresh in my mind when I got into the taxi and, since Cooper was going to spend life in prison, it seemed only right that I follow through with our engagement and empty a few beers in his name.

I sat down, ordered two bottles of Bud, and watched with amazement as Cooper came limping through the door. I thought, at first, that I was hallucinating; some sort of stress reaction. I stared, unbelieving, as he sat down and grabbed one of my beers.

It was early, and the bar was empty. I had no doubt that, if it had been full, people would be staring at my bloody friend. Thankfully, it was only the bartender and us.

The bartender regarded Cooper from across the bar. Then, in as casual a tone as I had ever heard, he said, "The bathroom's in back. We have paper towels. Clean up any blood you get on the sink." Cooper tipped an invisible hat to the man, then struggled to his feet.

When he came back the blood was gone. The cut beside his swollen, bruised, and bloodshot eye was wide and clearly in need of stitches, but it was not bleeding. His nose was angled differently than it had been that morning and his lip—swollen and purple—looked like a sausage resting on his chin . . . but there was no more blood.

Thank God for small miracles, I thought. *If I ever see blood again it will be too soon.*

Sipping my beer, I said, "What do you plan on doing now?"

I could not read his expression. His face was a bloated mask, and moving it—even slightly—seemed to cause him pain, so he spoke slowly. "Dunno . . ."

He finished his beer and slowly asked the bartender for four more. The bartender promptly handed him the beers, then moved away to a comfortable distance. Cooper handed one to me.

"I'm thinking about going with Michelle," he said, finally.

"That's a good idea."

"Yeah . . . can't really stay around here, can I?"

"No," I said, and finished the rest of my beer. Then

I finished the one that Cooper had given to me. The veteran bartender, anticipating my order, brought me two more.

"Definitely can't go back to PaperClips," Cooper said softly. "Not after killing my boss's boyfriend."

The bartender was on the phone, talking to what sounded like his girlfriend, or maybe his wife. Oblivious to our conversation, he heatedly discussed the results of a PTA meeting.

"Shh." I said, nervously lifting my finger to my mouth. "Some of us have to stay here."

"Yeah . . . listen buddy . . ." He paused, guzzled down his two remaining beers, and one of mine. "I best be going. I don't know when Michelle's flight leaves. If I mean to catch her, I should probably get to the getting. Know-mean?"

"Yeah," I said, and watched as he painstakingly peeled himself from the stool, and reached for his wallet. "No. No way. I got this one, Cooper. You get it next time."

Again, he tipped his imaginary hat; once to me, once to the bartender. "Much obliged, Chris. Suppose I'll be seeing you."

"Yeah, I suppose you will."

"I've got your address," he said. "Once I get things figured, I'll drop you a line."

"Yeah. Make sure you do. I'll be expecting it."

I rose from my seat, and we hugged. It was the kind of hug I used to give my brother when we were young. Firm, sincere, and loving. For a moment, I was tempted to kiss him on the cheek, but in the end, I refrained.

"See you around," I said, letting him go.

His hug lingered for a moment longer. Then, he too let go.

"Yeah," he said, gently wiping a tear from his swollen eye.

"I'll drop you a line."

He walked out the door. Then he was gone.

Chapter 34

Without thinking I checked the mail. Empty. Again.

Figures. I don't know why you thought it would be anything other than empty. Who the fuck are you kidding, Chris. There was never going to be any letter.

I could have killed myself then. This was easily the worst day of my life, and I was quickly losing faith. Not just in myself, but in the world too. In everything. Anything.

There was a bottle of wine in my fridge. The last gift from a friend that I would likely never see again. I could taste it. The heavenly fluid. It was waiting for me in my apartment. It was calling to me. I walked quickly up the stairs to meet it.

"You're home late."

Sofia—not waiting for me to fully open the door—
flung herself at me. I had not hugged her like this in a long
time. It felt familiar. It felt good. It felt safe. Mostly, it felt
honest.

She relinquished her weight to me, and I carried
her, in a hug, back over the threshold. We kissed our way
past the living room, and into the bedroom. Sofia jumped
up, and wrapped her legs around my waist. We kissed like
this for what seemed like years; spinning around the room
like a top-heavy ballerina.

Dizzy, I threw her onto our bed, and within moments we were naked.

I dove into her with such tremendous force that I
thought she might scream in pain. Instead, she moaned.

We made love for the first time in months. Starved
for the quake and electricity of orgasm, we stayed in bed for
hours. Until finally—sore and delirious with ecstasy—our
bodies demanded that we stop. Grudgingly, we remitted.

"You're home early," I said, as I kissed her ear.

"I finished the project that I've been working on. A
bunch of us were going to go to the bar, but there was an
accident on the A train. I don't know what happened
exactly, but they announced that the train would be out of
service until further notice. One of the girls from my office
had a sister who was there. Apparently, she said that
someone fell onto the tracks . . . right as the train was
coming." Sofia turned to me, and said, "Can you imagine
that? Falling on the tracks is one of my worst nightmares." I
closed my eyes, and tried desperately to block out the

memory of Vinny's terrified face. "So, I decided to skip the bar. I took a taxi home instead." She licked her finger and painted a line of moisture from the bridge of my nose to the tip. "Plus, I figured we deserved to do a little . . . catching up."

"I love you, Sofia. I don't say it enough, but I do. I love you. I love you a lot."

She kissed and climbed atop of me. Pushing through the pain, we made love until the consciousness left our bodies, and the dreams carried us away.

The next day we woke up late, and showered together. It had been so long, since we last shared such a moment, that I felt like a stranger discovering her body for the first time.

We lingered in the shower until we were both painfully pruned.

As usual, I was dressed first. So, kissing her on the neck, I offered to go buy food. "I'll be right back. I'm going to go and buy eggs and bacon. Maybe even some bagels and cream cheese . . ."

She giggled innocently, and asked, "Orange juice too?"

"Of course. Everything. I'm feeling decadent," I said, ending the sentence with a wet kiss to her cheek.

I was surprised that this was all it took. In less time than it took to unfold, I had forgotten about yesterday. It all seemed like it was only a nightmare. A nightmare that I was only too glad to forget.

I checked the mail on the way out. There was a pile, and I flipped through it quickly. Electric bill, phone bill, internet bill, credit card bill, credit card offer and then . . .

I ran upstairs. Sofia was dressed, and on the computer. I dropped all but one letter onto the floor. Then I grabbed Sofia by the wrist, and tugged. She hopped to her feet, and I dragged her—laughing—out of the door.

"What is this?" she said, in-between sharp little giggles.

"In a second," I said. "I want to go to the park."

"But, what about breakfast?" Amusement gave way, and was replaced by a look of utter panic. "I'm really hungry. Do you know how many calories I burned last night?" she asked.

"We'll go out to eat, Sofia. We'll go to Capital Restaurant on Broadway and get some pancakes and corned beef hash." She beamed at this exciting and unexpected good news.

"Now come on," I said, tugging her hand. "let's go."

The park was unseasonably warm. It felt like late summer rather than mid-fall. The sky was clear, save for a few happy clouds that passed casually along its surface. Brightly colored leaves danced in a gentle, warm wind that blew in from the Hudson River. I took off my jacket and placed it on the yellowing grass. Sofia sat, and I followed.

"Will you, finally, tell me what this is all about? I'll tell you right now . . . if you're planning to propose to me at Dyckman Fields the answer is no," she said through an "I'm just kidding" grin.

I told her that I was not going to propose. She pantomimed relief as I pulled the folded envelope from my pocket.

"I went to an open mic a while back," I began. "I read a short story of mine. I think you read it. 'The Kiss'?" She nodded, and said that she remembered it. "Well . . . to sign up to read, I had to give my contact information to the guy at the door. I didn't think anything of it at the time, but, the next day I got an email from a publisher."

She raised her hands, said, "Woo," and motioned for me to slow down. "Wait, what?" she asked, with a doubtful chuckle. "You went to a poetry reading?"

"Short story reading . . ." I corrected. "And, yes."

"Why didn't you tell me?" she asked. "I would have loved to have gone."

"Well, Sofia, we haven't exactly been the best communicators in the world . . . and besides, you were working. I only decided to go because you were working." Feeling a bit of the old resentment, I looked away.

She reached out and grabbed my hand. "I'm sorry, keep going. You got an email?"

"From a publisher. He said he liked my work. In the email he said he would like me to send him something longer."

"Your novel?" she asked.

"Yeah. I printed it the day I got hate-crimed."

"I remember that day. You spent the rest of the night getting drunk in the shower."

"Yeah . . ."

I held the letter up, handed it to her, and said, "This is his reply."

She looked at me, then at the bent envelope, then back at me. Obviously surprised at the enormity of what I was telling her, she said, "This seems like something that would have come up in conversation."

"And, when exactly was our last conversation, Sofia? We haven't talked in months. Literally, months. I only ever see you when you're sleeping. This is . . ."

She put a finger to my lips, and said, "I know. I'm sorry. I just take my job seriously. But . . . it's only because I want the future to be easier. I work hard now, so that later I can relax. So that later *we* can relax. I thought you knew that."

"I do. . . . I do. Honestly, Sofia, I do. It's just so hard to think about the future, when I miss you so much today." She came close and kissed me.

"I'm here now, Chris. I'm sorry about how things were. I'll try and make it better."

"Me too," I said.

We kissed for a long time, then I fell into her lap. She flipped me over, and I used her lap as a pillow.

I looked at the sky, and said, "Now, bust that letter open and give me the bad news."

She voiced a passable drumroll, and I zeroed in on a slowly rolling cloud. It was thick, and white. It was perfect; a cloud from a movie, or maybe a painting. I focused on it—hard. Attached myself to it. Whatever the news, no matter how bad it seemed, I would be okay. That cloud was at peace with the world, and, as long as I focused on it, I would be too.

The drumroll stopped, and Sofia began to read. In response, my breathing ceased, and my eyes involuntarily shut.

"Mr. Christian, we are very pleased to inform you that . . ." I reached up and grabbed her midsentence. I kissed her with a smile that stretched from ear to ear, and grabbed the paper from her and read the rest of the letter aloud.

For the second time, in as many days, I felt as though I was in shock.

Sofia collapsed into my arms, and began to weep.

After a long moment, I spoke the most delicious words that I had ever dared to utter. "Sofia, I am going to quit PaperClips."

Afterwards One:

I printed the first completed draft of my novel at PaperClips. I went in the afternoon, and Maria was only too glad to help me. She was doing well under a new manager. Eric had been fired for sexual harassment and labor violations.

Tiffany was forced to resign after the investigators charged with Eric's case unearthed video of her and the former manager engaged in "lewd behavior" on PaperClips premises. Maria had not seen either of them since.

Afterwards Two:

Months later, as Sofia and I prepared to move to a larger apartment in the Village, I received a postcard. It was a picture of a shirtless man, on a white beach, with a beautiful woman on each arm. The man looked familiar, but his face was obscured by the shadow of a large tan cowboy hat. I flipped it over.

Written in black marker on the back was this: "Greetings from Puerto Rico. Visit soon. Love Cooper."

Afterwards Three:

After everything, I rediscovered the package from Mexico. It was buried in the freezer, under a bag of frozen corn. I threw it in the trash without opening it.

Afterward Four:

This whole time, Sofia and I owned a dog named Baxter. Why—how—did he avoid making an appearance in this book? I have no clue. Clearly an oversight on my part. Sorry. I'll put a picture of him on the cover.

Hopeful

A novel

www.ingramcontent.com/pod-product-compliance
Lightning Source LLC
Chambersburg PA
CBHW021219250626
47155CB00008B/2877